The Logic
of the World

—————————⟫•⟪—————————

ROBERT KELLY

The Logic of the World

And Other Fictions

McPherson & Company

2010

THE LOGIC OF THE WORLD AND OTHER FICTIONS

Published by McPherson & Company,
Post Box 1126 Kingston, New York 12402,
with assistance from the Literature Program of the
New York State Council on the Arts, a state agency.
Designed by Bruce R. McPherson.
Typeset in Adobe Garamond and Galliard.
Printed on pH neutral paper.
Manufactured in the United States of America.

1 3 5 7 9 10 8 6 4 2   2010 2011 2012

LIBRARY OF CONGRESS CATALOGING-IN-PUBLICATION DATA

Kelly, Robert, 1935-
   The logic of the world and other fictions / Robert Kelly.
   p. cm.
   ISBN 978-0-929701-89-9 (hardcover : alk. paper)
   I. Title.
   PS3521.E4322L64 2010
   813'.54—dc22

                            2009047279

ACKNOWLEDGMENTS
Some of these fictions have been published in *Conjunctions, Blind
Spot, Five Fingers Review, Golden Handcuffs, Washington Square,
Annandale Dream Gazette, First Intensity* and *Golden Handcuffs*.
"The Wandering Jew" was privately printed as a greeting card.

Table of Contents

I

I I

I I I

IV

V

Forty Square Meters

SHE HAD MOVED INTO an apartment in the old part of the city. The street was so old it was there when Sadi-Carnot was assassinated, when the saxophone was invented, when Berlioz swept through the avenues openly crying for his lost Irish love. It was there when the king stopped for pork pudding at Varennes. It was there when the English burnt the girl they called Joan at Rouen. It was there when his angry in-laws crept up the stairs one night and castrated sleeping Abelard. It was there, but none of those things happened on her street.

No sooner did he get her postcard announcing the new address and its size, forty square meters, than he jumped on a plane and hurried to her place. She came home from the university to find him cross-legged on the landing outside her door, reading a book in the dim light.

—Your poor eyes, she said.

He reached up and caressed her hip, then holding onto her for leverage pulled himself to his feet.

—I'm here, he said.

They didn't try to kiss each other in the hallway. And the minute she'd let him in to her new apartment, he immediately lay down fully outstretched on the floor.

—See, he said, only two meters, not even that.

—What are you talking about? She wanted to know.

—You said in your card your place had only forty square meters, and here I am, plenty of room, I take up at the most two meters, that leaves thirty eight meters for you and everything else.

He stretched his arms over his head and closed his eyes. She came and sat down on the floor beside him. She was glad to see him, she liked him, but she wasn't sure if she liked him right there, on the floor, on his two meters. She was suddenly worried that already she was thinking about it as his two meters. Uh oh.

2

It wasn't long before all the space was filled.

She was so busy at the university, course work and preparations and reading, and keeping up with the language of the city, still new and challenging for her as an everyday activity, hearing and speaking and answering and begging and wanting and fearing, all out loud and every day all day, not just sometimes in her own country reading a book in it or listening to a song. She was busy most of every day, and she didn't really have time to worry too much about him being there. Maybe there really was enough room.

Sometimes when they made love she was on top of him, all on his two meters, or he was on top of her, and his two meters became her two meters, and they fit nicely into the space. Then she sometimes lay there with the cool linoleum of the floor against her shoulder blades and his weight pressing against her firmly. No matter what was happening they seemed to fit inside the space.

Often when they were just doing different things, he was reading, she was writing or revising, he would say:

—Come over and sit with me. And she would. Or he would say:

—Come sit on me. He was always wanting her to sit on him, and sometimes she would sit on his lap or his stomach, as if he were a log and she straddled him. Or she would be sitting down beside him and he would quickly slip his hand under her so she would find herself sitting on the palm of his hand.

—I could lift you to the sky, he said. I'm holding you as if you were a little bird, he said.

—I'm not comfortable, she said.

—So fly away, he said.

But she would go on sitting there, and they would talk till his hand grew numb under her, and her body forgot to feel she was sitting on anything special.

He didn't have much to say, actually, but he loved to listen to her.

—You speak more coherently than anyone I ever heard, you talk the way a keen brain must think, you notice everything, you balance everything, you analyze without harshness, you synthesize without blur.

He said things like that to her, he was always trying to describe to her the powerful beauty he found in the way she thought and the way she spoke. He must have felt that if he could tell her the effect she and her talk had on him it would somehow be a reward or an apology for making her talk to him all the time.

—You talk the way the wind investigates a flower, harming nothing, touching everything. You talk the way my own memories recall everything that ever happened to me, have you ever noticed that? Memory finds everything relevant, memory relates everything to its center of awareness, nothing is ever trivial if it is remembered — you talk like that, everything connects.

He would say things like that, truthfully, trying hard to get it right why he liked her so much. And he liked the sound of her voice.

—How old your voice is! It has been speaking from the beginning of the world!

He loved to listen to her, alert, alert. It wasn't good to drift off on the sound of her voice, no, he had to listen carefully. He liked listening carefully, because all the rest of him was so messy and approximate.

—I am approximate, and you are exact, he said to her. And he pulled her towards him so that he could nuzzle her between the legs. He repeated what he had said, but the words, true to their meaning, were muffled now. But she understood.

3

What did he do all day while she was at the university? There was much to interest him in the apartment, as we shall see. But after a few preliminary tours of inspection, picking up her clothes and holding them to his cheek, sometimes rubbing smooth cloth on his rough stubble, shamelessly reading through her notebooks, staring at his shadow against her wall, he would finally wander over to the window and look down at the rooftops and the noisy street and think about nothing. He hoped people would appear in all the windows, so many windows, a city is all about windows, the mystery of privateness so suddenly revealed, all it takes is a curtain swept aside by the busy wind, a shade rolled up, a light switched on, a flare of lightning on a hot night. We are private so we can show. We wear clothes so we can take them off. If he was think-ing at all, his thoughts were like that, slow images of bod-ies seen quick in the windows, in the street, in the sky. All the places we don't belong.

Soon enough he would go down the many stairs and spend the day in the streets. Looking at people, talking to them in some language they could cobble together from whatever languages people know, people always know something. He would walk around for hours, looking at bookstores trying to find one with his own books in the window. But how many bookstores sold Swedish books? Even though two of his books had been translated, *The Silja Gull* and *Time on a Leash*, he didn't see them in any window, though one or two shops had them inside, on the shelves in their proper place.

He would eat things he'd buy in shops, a little wheel of pale runny cheese he'd eat from his hand, and leave what he didn't want on the park bench, a litre of milk, a bag of black cherries. Then he'd walk some more, and buy some food to bring home to cook for dinner. He'd carry that in a little nylon mesh bag he'd had in his pocket all along.

.   .   .

4

Later they would both be home. She accepted him. She would stand at the window in her turn now, evening light, and let him stand beside her, his arm around her. Sometimes he would be a child and let his head rest on her shoulder.

He has such a heavy head, she thought. But her head was large too, generous with thought and remembering.

And then she would let her head rest on his shoulder. Not very long, just a little while, long enough as if to say I love you too.

Mostly though they kept busy in the apartment. There was so much to do.

The thirty-eight meters had almost all been taken up.

She kept two meters for herself, right near the window, where she could sleep alone when she was annoyed at him or bored with him. Most nights they slept together. But it is good to have space of one's own.

She kept another three meters for her school work, desk and chair and slim bookcase wedged against the wall and overflowing up the wall towards the distant ceiling. So much work for her, at the desk and in the books.

So much work for her too talking to him, listening at him. Then he might suddenly need her to jump up from whatever she was doing so she could hold his book open in front of him while he practiced a posture of ancient Peruvian Inca yoga that was described in the book, or else he needed, suddenly, right now and not a moment later, to smell her hair, to smell the roots of her hair, where (he said) her hair grows out of thinking, I love your thinking.

ſ

They had brought all kinds of things into the apartment from the outside world. Once you get a big thing through the door, it can fit in surprisingly small space — that's what they discovered.

Saturdays they would spend wandering around, finding things for their apartment. The thirty-three meters left unoccupied seemed by now a vast desert, full of challenge.

Several months had passed, and not once had he suggested that he might leave, or get a place of his own, or a life of his own, or go back to his own country, never once, after several months this is what they had in the apartment:

One meter contained the whole of Mount Kilimanjaro, which came from Africa. It was so high that there was always snow on top of it, right up almost touching the ceiling. When it got hot and stuffy in the apartment, they would climb high up the gentle slopes of the mountain till they found a cool grotto, where lush vegetation welcomed them, and they listened to the springs gurgling down into basalt basins and leopards coughing in the woods, and they watched cute little hyraxes tumbling and playing and nibbling seeds.

Right next to that mountain, a square meter contained a small meadow on the slopes of the Donnersberg, not far from the Rhine. On it a few dozen cows, slim but big-uddered, wandered, sunlight warming their café-au-lait colored pelts. These cows provided them with fresh milk for their coffee and cereal, with enough left over to make quark and soft white cheese.

They spent (or wasted, she sometimes thought) two whole meters on Lake Mono, the third oldest lake on the planet Earth, it is said. They brought it from California. Deep and very blue, it was extremely salty, good for floating, but the rim of the lake was pure white with sun-dried salts. The waters were healing, perhaps, but they were not especially refreshing.

So they spent another meter on an intimate Alpine lake they ordered from the Graubünden. But that turned out to be too cold for all but the hottest days of August when even the crowded street outside was struck dumb by the sun. Then the lake would please them. At other times, they mostly liked it for the thunderstorms that massed above it so often, and blazed with lightning. On serene afternoons, gulls would float over it, very small and far away, like the gulls in his book over some lake back in Sweden.

One chaste, even austere, meter was devoted to the several volumes of the great Littré dictionary, stacked up, and on it she would sometimes perch for hours, thinking, dreaming often of her own homeland and her distant friends. It would be months still before she could go home.

In the meantime, they were together. How long would they be together? What does that mean? He had his two meters, she had her five meters, and that's what the world is like.

—We are born alone and we die alone. She said that to him once, severely, she forgot why she said it, but it was true. It is true.

But they seemed to be now, and seemed to be together, and lived in this apartment where all kinds of things had been gathered. It is a pleasure to live in a world like this.

Because they had lots of things and circumstances, things and textures to live with. This is what they had accumulated so far, each thing on its own square meter or maybe a little more:

1. A Blaupunkt table-model radio from 1955, with a sleek rank of plastic pushbuttons and huge plastic knobs that by now had taken on the look of old ivory and were good to feel. It made sound still, but they quarreled about what music was to listen to, and he would begin to lecture on the evils of this and the virtues of that. Mostly they used it to listen to the news, he didn't understand the language all that well, and then she'd have to explain to him what they'd just heard.

2. An armchair they had found in the street. He had, for sanitary reasons, sprayed it with a powerful disinfectant, of which it still smelled so strongly that nobody liked to sit in it. Still, it was nice to drop full shopping bags on, or pile books up on, or toss clothes when you took them off.

3. A bath-tub occupied two of the meters. It had feet in the shape of lion claws, but a peculiar lion, because the feet at one end of the tub pointed in one direction, while the feet at the other pointed in the other. With all the lakes in the room, it didn't get used much for baths, but it was an excellent space for storing clothes, since they didn't have to be folded, hence didn't get wrinkled.

4. A tobacco stand, whose central storage area was lined with copper. Neither of them smoked. The stand had a cactus living on it that never got watered and never died.

5. A metal-stamping factory that made economy-grade scissors and shears from sheet metal. The workmen were all Japanese, and the bouncy jive of that emphatic language could be heard all day long in that part of the room.

6. A small railroad town from Pennsylvania, on the shore of the Delaware River, one elbow of which—shallow, slow, green with summer—can be seen just at the edge of the town. On the one street, a train is idling, taking on water and dropping off two worried-looking passengers. No one has come to meet them at the station. In a little diner, a girl is ordering pancakes, but you have to bend very low to hear her, so shy is she that her voice is low, if musical.

7. A beech tree.

8. A little wild boar shoat, his furry back still dappled with the pale fawn-spots of very young swine. He took up very little space, though some space, wherever it was. But it tended to move around quite a lot, the way younger animals do, even though it normally tended to gravitate back to the tree, from which beechnuts would presently begin to fall.

9. A little country church from Bavaria. Its steeple, onion-bulbous at the base, narrowed to a very pointy summit, tipped with a simple Latin cross like the protective button on an épée—the cross kept him and her from scratching themselves on the sharp spire.

10. An old waterless fountain from Sicily. The stone was rust-stained and crumbly, and the stonework looked as if it had been made a thousand years ago by Arabs, but who can say. Waterless, in general, yes. But every once in a while, often in the middle of the night, or in a silent afternoon after love siesta, they would suddenly hear a trickle, and they would sleepily look into the fountain and see a little gush of water up, just an inch or two above the old lead pipe from which the spray once rose. Enough water would come out to cover most of the basin, then

the flow would stop. Sometimes he or she, or the two of them together, shoulder to shoulder, or even closer, hip to hip, arms around each other, would kneel at the rim of the fountain and bend forward, holding each other, and drink from the strange and sudden water, that always tasted like metal or tasted like stone, they could never decide. In the morning, sometimes the basin would still be damp to the touch.

And even so there was always room for more.

Baby

WILL THEY BE WAITING for the Child who's just been born? Do they have something planned for the christening, the party, the salty afters when they try to put the infant to sleep and get on with their lives?

"Sleep twenty years or so," the parents think. "Sleep until we wake, ready for your famished caresses, your trivial ideas."

I am the child. I am lying alert but silent in the yummy arms of my nurse, who will soon carry me to the church. I am busy paying attention to the firm softness of her arms, the maddening bottomless softness of her breasts, both of which I contrive to rest against.

My parents and the priest are busy doing what they always do: talking nonsense by the shovelful, praying to false gods, planning for a future that will never be theirs.

I am the future. I am god.

Because I am quiet and gently peeing in my clothes, I can hear them think. Anybody can hear them talk, but I hear them thinking. I can measure by this means their sincerity, and rate them on a scale of one to ten: Mother 9.5, Father 4.7, Priest 0.3. So much for kings, bishops, and the way things are.

I am the new way that things are.

Peeing gently really lets you hear them thinking. Try it before you forget. Releasing sphincters releases everything.

Every story is a sort of coming. I will probably forget this later, so I want to stress it now, before we lose sight of this important—perhaps the most important—physiological peculiarity of ours. We think by coming, we tell by uttering, we utter by outing, we out by letting go. Whee! the nursemaid says.

She is cute, and already I want to do things with her. But what can I do? It is frustrating. I can't walk, even, and can't talk so that she understands, and my godly prong is still little, little, though just at this moment it's hard as a peach pit and wants to probe.

All I can do is touch her skin. She smiles down or up at me, depending, and accepts this dim signal, symbol, of what I really want. Even now I touch her where I can, my little paws bunching against the skin of her breasts that shows above her modest blouse.

And I am after all resting on her intimate friendly nurturing melodies right and left, one of them dribbling a little bit just out of reach of my patrolling tongue.

These constraints! These restrictions I've just been so freely acknowledging, they must make you think that if

I'm god, as I say and do believe, I must be a pretty feeble kind of god.

Perhaps. But what do we really know? About gods or anything else for that matter. What do we know about the powers of gods? Maybe their only power is in making fathers and mothers and bishops and nursemaids wait on them hand and foot. Let us recognize (even the anthropologists do) by the fact of cult that a god is being worshipped. Incense and processions and people acting strange: there is true power, to make sensual men and women act so weirdly. Men and women of flesh bow down and worship an unseen idea, how strange that is. Worship me!

Surrounded though I am by these Ordinary Worshippers (parents and clergy and ministrants) and Automatic Enemies (the siblings I gather have come this way before me, and doubtless lie in wait for me even at this moment), I am really only interested (after all, there's plenty of time for these aforementioned geezers and malcontents) in the Unseen Many who may deem it fit to show up at my baptism.

I hope someone has taken the precaution of inviting them. I know how easy it is to do that, but these silly Talking People around me have probably forgotten how it's done. The glass of milk poured out on the doorstep at midnight; the piece of bread with a lighted candle shoved in the crumb that's let burn down from dusk of the day before; the spider dropped on the nursemaid's breast; the iron bar left in running water two weeks before the christening—any of these work perfectly well. Each suffices to bring the Pale Hard-to-See People I am anxious to have at my ceremony.

I want them to bless me, if possible, or curse me if not. Any contact with them is productive of Difference, and, let's face it, difference is what we came into this Vale of Tears hot to have, hot to feel, peel, prong, prod, tingle, mingle, shove it in. Or sit down in it, and watch the stars spin across the staggering sky.

Blessing, of course, is what I want most. The blessing that I won't ever forget anything I know now or will come to learn. That I can speak all languages of women, and some of men. That I won't forget the instant when they come and put their special salt on the spitty tip of my tongue and I taste it ever after. I will always be thirsty, I promise, I promise.

Looking up at her soft, idle, unfocussed mouth, I let myself pee freely. I will always. I promise myself that I will come inside her—sooner than you think, skeptic sinners—come inside her or someone just as good, or better, or not quite. Someone I will enter in the night and stay rigid in till the rising of the dawn, just like the man in the bible who strove all night with a Man. No man for me, though, I'm man enough for me. Just give me this shapely brook full of stars that runs through the snug confinement of her clothes. O a woman's body is a river into which I fain would plunge, lust, lust. But nothing to be done about it yet.

Soon, soon they'll come, the ones who talk without moving their lips and stand unseen—but I will see them —all round me while the senile bishop tries to drown me and my godparents—dukes and duchesses they seem to be, fat fools is what I see—mumble mumble mumble promises they won't keep in an ancient language they don't understand and I will try to forget.

Soon they will be there, all round me, the ones I wait for, I feel a certainty stirring in me now like the first bowel movement of the new day, I feel the pressure of certainty, I know they'll be there. Even their curse would keep me different from all others, make me lame or mute or prone to sprout wicked little horns above my eyebrows. Whatever it is, blessing or curse, I know that they will never let me forget what I know now, this princely world so full of faces, all of them for me. All the pain is for me, and all the pleasure also is mine.

Whether it hurts me or caresses me, it's all for me. I delight in the rich regency of silence that will be mine until these foolish Visible People make me talk and take Communion and learn fractions and lists of kings my ancestors.

Years yet before I have to worry about that. Now the years are for me, years of castles and spindles and cherries and distaffs and milk, milk, milk.

Crucifixes

THERE WAS AN OLD WOMAN who told a little boy
about how God died. Her face was white. He never
had seen such white skin. He thought: she has no blood.
Where has all her blood gone?

She was old, but he had seen other people who were
old or older. She lived upstairs in a small apartment house
made of pale yellow brick. It was on the corner of the
last block before the vacant lots. He didn't like apartment
houses. Old people lived in them.

Her apartment was clean, she was so white, he was
afraid.

Children are terrible. They get frightened and don't
care. Anxiety and alienage and difference and terror, these
drive out compassion. Mostly children don't have any
compassion.

The poor old woman in her clean apartment and clean cotton housecoat and fluffy white hair and no color in her face. The poor old woman. But he didn't feel that.

He felt only fear and distance. First it was just the ordinary fear, the one he carried with him, close as the sweaty skin on his neck, and that woke up and made him hot and breathless, when he met new people, or old people, or his mother told him to say something to somebody, say something, talk, show them how much you know.

But then as this white woman began to talk to him, showing him all the things she knew, he began to develop a new kind of fear. This kind didn't seem to be his own. It seemed to be a fear or fright in the nature of things, like a snake beneath a hedge (but he liked snakes) or a panther in the underbrush. It was there, not here, but it could come out at any moment and seize him and destroy him, till there was nothing left but the fear.

How had he gotten here? It was summer. His aunt had taken him. She was in her pale lavender cotton dress, and she was almost as pale as the scary lady, her white fluffy old hair too. She carried her parasol, she took him by the hand and brought him to visit her friend.

The old women sat and drank tea and talked a long time and left him alone while he read in the Bible. This was interesting. This woman had a Bible, the whole one. At home they had only the New Testament. Here was the whole thing, and he was happy. He read in it. He liked reading in Leviticus, where there were doves, and where walls could have leprosy, and where the priests moved among ordinary people saying things he wanted to understand. It was interesting. Doves were like pigeons, houses still had walls, his father had claimed to see Chinamen with leprosy bundled out of stifling laundries into the black wagon to be carted away forever. Here were things he understood, still with us, heaven and earth. Things of the earth. Pigeons outside this very window wheeling in the sky above where the trolley car turned around its big circle at Avenue U to come back north up Nostrand.

By now the old women were finished with their tea and crumb buns and had given him one too, he was always hungry, they always made fun of him for being hungry. But what is there to do with the world except eat it, take it in, by eye, ear, mouth, touch? Wasn't he here in this garden to take it all in?

The women began talking to him. Why are you reading the Bible, the owner of the Bible wanted to know. The boy said something. What can he say, it's interesting. He doesn't want her to know how interesting he finds it— he knows the Bible is true, and here are hundreds of pages of true things for him to read and remember. What can he say?

Why wasn't he reading the New Testament, he wasn't a Protestant, was he, this little boy? No. He tried to tell the woman that they had a New Testament at home and he could read it whenever he liked, but that it wasn't very interesting. Besides, it seemed to be just about Church, while the Bible seemed to be about the whole world. But he couldn't say these things, he didn't know how. He knew how to feel differences, but not how to say them.

You should read about Our Lord, the old woman said. You should learn how He suffered for us, and what they did to Him. Do you know?

The boy didn't know. He knew Our Lord died on the cross—everybody knew that, and you could see it in every church, Jesus on the cross. But the boy didn't know how Jesus got there.

So the woman told him.

There was a big garage up Flatbush Avenue built right into a building, big wide entrance broad enough for a dozen cars. And up one side of the entry bay was a long ramp that cars could drive, up into the interior of the building, though he had never seen a car do so.

This is what he saw now as the woman explained how Jesus was tortured. Thorns were pressed into his face and ears and sunburned neck as the thorny branches and stalks were wrapped tightly around his head. Then or before, he was beaten with rods and sticks. Things were stuck into him here and there. Maybe his hair turned white from pain. Maybe he cried. Now and then he was whipped with a cat of nine tails. Do you know what that is, the woman wanted to know.

No, he didn't know. He knew enough to guess that it wasn't a real cat. It's a whip, they are whips, nine thin rawhide whips with sharp iron nails tied into the thongs to make them rip the skin not just hurt it. Would you like to feel that? No, he wouldn't like that.

And then they made him climb the hill to Calvary.

A hill. The only hill he could think of was the ramp in the garage, so up that oily, interesting smelling slope the doomed man in his rags was pushed and dragged by the brutal Romans and the sneering Jews and the weakling disciples couldn't do a thing to help. The Son of God was this man battered and bleeding and stinking and sweating and dragging his hundred pound cross up the hill surrounded by the jeering multitudes o Lord.

But what he saw was Jesus alone, in white rags, blood-soaked to be sure, but all alone, bent low as if he were carrying a great weight, a rock or body or a cross, but no cross was to be seen. Just poor Jesus bent low in bloody white rags shuffling quietly up the concrete ramp all slick with grease. All alone, in the shadowy recesses of the garage, while traffic clipped along behind him on Flatbush Avenue. He heard a trolley rush by. Once, near the top of the ramp, Jesus turned his head and looked at him.

This look was too much for the boy, and he began to cry. His aunt said to her friend, now you've made him cry, and he never cries.

The boy went on crying quietly, snuffling, not sobbing, really. Soon enough his aunt stood up and gathered her pocketbook and parasol and then they walked home. She never talked while they walked.

From that day forward, for many years the boy could not bear the sight of a crucifix in a house. It is strange, it never frightened him in the church. Nothing is real in a church, and you expect to see strange things there anyhow—candles when nobody used candles anymore, gold when you couldn't have gold in your house, mosaic walls when your walls were paint and plaster. So the crucifixes were strange but safe. Besides, the big crucifix over the altar had a Jesus wearing clothes, a long purple robe, and instead of a crown of thorns he had a real golden crown, like the king in "Prince Valiant."

But in the dark apartments of his aunts, he had so many uncles and aunts, in their dark tunnel-like railroad flats or their brick houses with chilly sunporches, to walk through a bedroom or a kitchen and see it there, that thing, that agony on the wall, looking at him, that was very frightening.

And they always did look at him, the Jesuses on the wall.

He wouldn't go into a room with a cross on the wall if he knew it was there. Or if he had to, he would hurry past it, his shoulder turned to the crucifix, going through the room as fast as he could, keeping an eye on it yet not wanting to see it. And sometimes he would just stand outside the door, trembling with fear.

The worst was in another aunt's bedroom, his favorite aunt. Her cross was huge and dark, a yard tall of blackened oak, with a metal figure on it that looked, because all one color and that not the color of human skin, like the terrible lepers he had heard about, dull silvery and cold. That cross he could never brace himself to meet.

They hid it when he and his mother came to visit. Then he could walk through the room.

Then one day he thought: where did they hide it? And instantly he knew, from the size of the thing, that there was only one place they could have put it when they took it down off the wall. He could see the hook still up there.

Under the bed. That's where they put it. That's where it was right now. Under the bed and looking out at him. Ready to come out, like a horrible bird from under the bed, ready to come to him. When he thought that, it was the worst fear he had ever felt in his life. He made no sound. He didn't whimper or let anybody know, anymore, ever, how frightened he was. He hurried into the bright living room where already his kindly uncle was at the piano beginning to pound out the jazz, stride, his big left hand prancing like a machine along the keyboard, while the boy sat trying to keep his fear to himself.

The Example of the Hawk

O UTSIDE A SMALL VILLAGE in Sicily stood a seldom-used fountain. Once a sprawling family had their houses all around it, but time and domestic quarrels and a lunatic grandson with a firebrand had left the fountain all alone at the center of this open space, sparsely littered with rubble, that once had been the square of the hamlet. Some people still liked to walk a few minutes out from the village to use its waters, reputed to have curative properties. Undeniably the water was tinged with a pale ruddy color, arguing iron in the soil through which it passed to rise and slip listlessly into the broad shallow basin built, no one knew how long ago, of rough yellow stone.

On the rim of this fountain one day a woman was sitting. She was fond of the spot since this was a place where she could usually be alone. She was alone now. The old stones of the fountain coping, worn round from years of washerwomen and children playing, were warm from the sun, and the sky above was vivid early evening blue, without even a single cloud.

The woman felt her body, it seemed, more vividly here than anywhere else. The stone against her thighs, the drift of her own warm hair over her bare warm arm, the quiet flurry of water behind her, the occasional nuzzling of wind against her cheek. It was hot, hot the way the south is hot, with a heat that does not surprise anybody. However fierce it may be, the heat seems part of the day, and the body seems part of the heat too, and so there is deep kinship. There is peace. And when there is peace there is feeling. Even when someone is very hot, it is a feeling. A sensation.

She was hot. She leaned back and stared up into the empty sky. It was a pleasure to do that. What a strange city the sky was! Sometimes busy as can be with clouds and birds and hailstones and dirty yellow dust storms from Africa, sometimes utterly deserted. The streets of the sky, she thought, and she liked that thought, and leaned back further, edging back a little on the stone.

Lazily she was aware of being dangerously close to falling back into the water. Instead of retreating, though, she felt bold, and with a tiny little thrill sat back even further. Now it was hard to keep from falling back. She had to clutch the edge of the fountain with her calves and knees, and hold the rim tight with her fingers. Otherwise she was almost suspended above the water. She liked the feeling of risk, liked it, liked the risk, risk makes us alive, risk makes the present truly present, so she decided to edge back a little further, if she could. To see what would happen. All at once she felt the water sudden, sudden, lapping against her skin. One moment she was dry and now she was wet. How quickly, totally, conditions change. A moment ago she was just like anybody else, but now she was a woman being soaked by the fountain. Even now she could have pulled forward and escaped, but she liked this dear risk, liked the soft feel of the water lapping at her, the cool hand of the water caressing her.

Now she was half in the water, and what could she do? At some point she would have to leave this lovely, lonely fountain and go home. How could she walk home through the village half-soaked like that? How could she explain it? It would be easier if she were completely wet, wouldn't it, easier to have fallen into the fountain, anyone can fall, all kinds of excuses abound. It would be safer to be completely wet. If she was wet all over, then no one would know that once the water had been touching her. A little water is a dangerous thing. Furthermore, she would like to be all in the water, like to feel what it would be like to be herself, fully clothed, but in the water. In the quiet street of the water.

So gripping the rim tightly with her knees, she released her hands from the stone, and slipped back into the water. Then she let go of the rim with her legs, and slid to the bottom of the basin.

The water that had been a tender caress was now a storm of everywhere at once. No part of her was untouched by its presence, a storm, a quiet storm. It was like yielding to the timid touch of a bashful lover, then finding yourself not hours later but instantly in the wild tumult of love-making, moaning in the sweaty bed.

But it was quiet in the water, and that pressure on her

ears was not sound; though it felt like sound, it did not sound like sound. She was happy where she was, and opened her eyes.

And that opening of the eyes seemed to her the naughtiest thing she had yet done, she thought the schoolgirl word, because one thing her mother had always insisted upon was keeping one's eyes closed in the water. The woman was sure her poor mother had kept her eyes closed when making love too. Or being made love to. Men doing useful things were allowed to keep their eyes open—men diving for sponges, fishermen releasing tangled nets, boys diving to recover the crucifix that the half-witted old priest solemnly tossed in the harbor every St. Peter's Day, a ceremony only boys could take part in, but that only girls seemed to understand.

She opened her eyes and looked up at the water. All she could do was see through the water, the same blue sky, and in between her eyes and the sky the long tendrils of her own hair were floating and tangling. She watched, and was afraid, and liked all she felt, and liked the pressure of the water on her ears and nostrils, the way the water suddenly lifted and lightened the limbs of her body, and touched her secret places and public places with equal precision, equal cool attention. She liked the feeling of her fear.

As she looked at the water, her hair, the day, the light, the sky, she saw something that wasn't herself and wasn't light—a dark movement somewhere up there, she could not tell how far, up there and up there, a small dark swift movement that tended to circle and swoop, and she knew it was a bird.

Though the bird was just a bird, and the bird was far, she understood she was no longer alone. Even under the water, she felt hot with embarrassment. Quickly she pulled herself to her feet and stepped out of the fountain. Water gushed from her, and her clothes clung pleasantly to her body, cool in the hot air to which she had been restored. She sat back down on the rim of the fountain again to dry a little in the sun, and looked up to observe the bird.

A hawk it was. A hawk wheeling above her. Somewhere invisible but not far, there must be some poor snake stretched drowsy on a rock, or some luckless rat nibbling at the rich-seeded toppled head of a sunflower. She wondered what the hawk's prey would be, and whether she should do anything about it. But what can one do?

Then as she watched, the bird paused in its circling and stooped suddenly down, straight towards her. She had never seen a hawk dive towards a human being, never heard of it, and thought it must be some trick of the late afternoon light, and that the bird was not coming to her, not at all.

But after all, the bird was coming to her, who knows why, and with a weight and solidity that shocked her, the hawk landed on her knee and dug lightly its very sharp talons into her leg. The tiny fierce pains, which quickly became one single pain, in the leg, the shock and startlement, all those did not manage to make the woman leap up and shriek and run, or beat the bird away. Instead, she sat there, with tears of pain coming to her eyes, shocked without sadness, and watched this strange heavy busy flustered unsmooth hawk that had just pounced on her from the sky.

And the hawk looked back, with the crazy eye that all birds have, but hawks and eagles most of all. The mad face looked at her, as a bird has to look, one eye at a time.

2

At a table in a dingy room, a man was sitting, elbows propped on the littered tabletop, his hands supporting his chin as he read a book in front of him. He had just finished reading a story called "The Example of the Hawk." Northern light came amply through the window beside him, though already it was after eight in the evening. He had finished his little supper.

What the woman in the story felt, all those sensations —that is what he wanted to do, make people feel. Not feel with the dim Aristotelian emotions, but feel, the way skin and eyes and noses and fingers feel. Real feelings. He wanted to make people feel.

He was an actor, and he had come to hate his work. Instead of the real feelings he wanted to give people, he could only give them weary, used-up old emotions, attitudes, and, worst of all, shallow momentary experiences. Experiences!

He read the parts of the story again that pleased him so: the pressure of the stone on her legs, the lapping of the water against her skin, the sensation of pressure all round, the sight of her own hair floating vague, like sea monsters, between her and the sun. That is what art was about, to make us feel like that, to feel really.

And that is just what the theater could not do. Night after night he would stand on the noisy stage in front of the eager audience, he was good enough as an actor, he was good, he would shout and whisper and insinuate and lie grandly, the grand good lies of the ancient playwrights, Racine, Marivaux, Lope, the clever not-so-good lies of his own time, Scribe, Brieux, and these new Scandinavians one heard of everywhere. But nowhere in all that, nowhere in all the theater that he knew, was there any way of making people actually feel. Or if they did feel, then what they felt was what they felt all the time anyhow, the smoky air of theater auditoriums, the itchy warmth of wool, the rubbery smell of umbrellas.

He read the story again now from the beginning to the end. There were parts in it he didn't care much about, the stuff about her mother, a rat eating a flower, they meant nothing to him. But the rest was wonderful — a woman was living in her body, living in her feelings. And her feelings were living in the world, in water and sun and air—her feelings belonged to the world! That's what the theater should do, give people such intensity of feelings as that woman, all alone, discovered in her fountain.

That is what he wants the theater to do. But how can it do it? Again and again he came to the same dead end in his thinking. Morose, he toyed with the remnants of his supper, breadcrumbs and spilled wine. He rolled the crumbs together and made them into a ball, squeezed them, a tight little ball of crumb, then rolled the bread ball across the table into the little pool of spilled wine. He watched the bread begin to absorb the wine. The wine got paler as it spread through the bread, the pinkish bread grew softer, the ball expanded and lost its integrity as it grew.

Bread and wine, he thought disgustedly. We live in a religion that wants to turn bread into the body of God. He jumped up from the table and snarled to the patient, dusty air of his cluttered room, "I want to turn bread into bread!" He wanted to make real things real to real people.

Not emotions but motions. Not ideas but actions. Not thoughts but sensations. All the rest is the twaddle of philosophy, religion, law. These phrases were saying and saying in him. And then inside him it said: The world is no bigger than our bodies. Not emotions but motions. The theater has to move. He sat back down at the table, convinced that this time he might be able to think it through.

He remembered once saying to a friend those very words: the theater has to move. And the friend said but oh yes, of course it does, and it does, I come out of a play tremendously moved, my feelings wrung dry, my heart palpitating, my whole being transported! And the actor had shaken his head, doubting the power of any words to make clear his own utter disappointment with that kind of movement—the friend was moved but never touched, transported but not transformed. What good was all that? What good were feelings? They pass away and leave no trace. But a touch! A body remembers a touch forever.

The actor thought so, at least, because he tended to locate himself, orientate himself in his life, by what amounted to a system of remembered physical sensations—this hand, that stone, her arm, that flower, that black dog grabbing his ankle firmly without breaking the skin. And he was sure that deep down every human was like that. All the talk of feelings was at best a code for sharing with others the news of those sensations, and at worst a dehydration of human experience into lifeless, wordy categories. Even the deepest grief was a real stone you felt you carried the real weight of in your chest.

Why couldn't the theater do to the audience what the world did to the woman in the story? Why can't the theater touch? Why can't the theater pounce down out of the sky and sit on your knee and dig its talons delicately into your real skin?

Somewhere in all this confusion of thinking, the actor felt that two notions stood out. He heard them humming in his head, a demand and a question, and he let them wheel slowly in his mind while he watched the sopping bread, which had finished its work of absorbing as much wine as it could. The lump of breadcrumb seemed to sprawl in a dry territory surrounded by what still was wine. The grain of the wood gleamed freshly, as if new-polished; all the old history of the wood was there, suddenly clean and visible, ruddy gleaming under the slim moisture of the wine. And the two notions went on curving their way through the actor's mind: The theater has to move. And why can't the theater touch?

Then quietly, quietly, the answers began to come to him. Moving means so many things, but mostly it means going somewhere. He saw a theater, the whole preposterous Italian architecture of it, awkwardly heaving to its knees and crawling down a boulevard, saw it leaving the city, shouldering its way through the narrow mediaeval gates and actually toppling them, sending the old stones sprawling everywhere, no need for cities, no need for governments and institutions, this is enough, this is the theater of the world, and it is coming to its own, it is the theater that is coming to the world, make room! Make room! The theater is on its way!

He saw the huge theater lumbering, but with a certain elegance about the skirts and elbows, lumbering through the forest, startling the wild boars and the tiny hedgehogs, and the screaming crows cheered it on. He laughed to see it in his mind's eye, the marvelous huge building soldiering on up mountainsides and through humid valleys, and everywhere it went it touched the people and changed them.

But it couldn't touch. The vision faded, his smile faded. The theater in the forest could touch the audience no more than it could in the Boulevard des Italiens. It would bring a novelty to the rustics, something to experience, but it would not touch. Do not confuse the export of interesting experience with the communication of real sensation—he thought that, severely, and the theater shimmered out of existence in his mind's eye, and left only the forest.

Why can't the theater touch the people in the audience? Because there are too many of them. The theater does not have that many hands. *One mind suffices for a thousand hands*, he remembered that line from that tiresome play of Goethe that professors always wanted actors to perform, and he thought sadly: I have the mind, but I do not have the hands.

Then he thought: but I do have hands, I have two strong hands, two long legs, a body and a soul. I do have hands, and I will touch them. I will be the theater, and I will touch them. The theater will move and the theater will touch.

3

That is how the famous Caravan of the Seven Stars was born, that for so many years was a familiar sight throughout Europe. Towns vied for its visits.

The actor put all his savings together, borrowed money from his old father the physician, sold a small farm he had inherited, and bought a fine sturdy wagon and a team of four coal-black horses. He spent a lot of the money on making his wagon taller and wider, decorating it inside and out, and buying elegant tack for his horses, silver cockades on each of them, and two full sets of harnesses, one with bells for day and one without for night. It pleased him to move silently as he could through the night, with only the coach lantern glowing weirdly on the roof of the green caravan.

Many a traveling theater had made its way through the little towns of France, Germany, Bohemia and the south, setting up in the afternoon and performing at moonrise and creaking away before noon the next day.

But this theater was different, would always be different. When it came to a town, it stayed and stayed until all the people who wanted to come to the theater had come, and sometimes come again. Then and only then did it move on.

The actor had solved his problem, he thought, in the most direct way. The ancient Greeks had developed the thing we call theater (theater: a way of looking) by isolating one member of the singing and dancing chorus, and having him represent a character in the story they were telling. So small a step it was from telling a story to enacting the story. Now the actor proposed to reverse that, or rather turn it inside out in a way that would transform the world. Now the theater would look at the audience.

His idea worked out simply. One by one the audience would enter the theater. One by one they would be exposed to the story inside the theater. One by one they would be informed by all the story had in it to touch them. One by one they would be touched. He would touch them. He touched them.

It was as simple as that. The actor would stand out-side the theater at evening, or in the golden afternoon of feast days, and surround himself with posters, objects, fascinating weapons and devices of the kind in those days called 'philosophical instruments'—telescopes, armillary spheres, theodolites, microscopes. Accompanying himself on the mandolin, he would sing a little song to the people of Ratzeburg or Pesaro or Thonon, he made the song him-self, and it would serve to beckon them into the theater, and serve to make his voice familiar to them, so that when they heard it again, in the dark dream inside the theater, they would deeply somehow be reassured. They would think: it is the pale man with the mandolin, the man with grey eyes, the man with a lisp, the man with hair in his eyes, the man with the German accent, the man with the long funny shoes. They would not worry so much at what happened to them.

But what happened to them? Whatever it was, it hap-pened one by one.

That was the genius or delusion, it is not yet decided, the genius or delusion of the actor. Turning two thousand years of theatrical history upside down, he made the au-dience into a single person at a time, confronted by the overwhelming place and sound and voice and person called the theater.

What happened inside? In the first years of the theater, the actor would, in his capacity of doorman, show each member of the audience into the theater, that is, into the wagon itself. Four steps up, and into a dark enclosure a dozen feet long, seven feet wide, high enough for most men to stand up in without brushing the roof. Dark in-deed, and full of things. Things with texture and temperature to them, things that made noise when you touched them, or that would leave a funny feeling on the back of your hand as you brushed by.

The actor would talk, using several voices, and tell some story full of images and sensations, and move around the visitor as he did so, touching, breathing, whispering. Sometimes there would come a sudden light, when the actor or an assistant slipped open the metal door of a dark-lantern, and the gleam would dazzle the eyes. It was light, and in this light people saw nothing—their eyelids clenched, they turned away from the light, and into the complex of sensations all round them. And all the while the actor talked.

People, one says. But there was only one member of the audience at a time. That was the hard thing to explain, to understand, and later to endure. When each person came out, alone as he had gone in, he would talk to some previous visitor, but often could find no common ground to their talk. Each seemed to experience a different world inside the theater. What to call such a person, who comes alone into the theater, hears, feels, beholds, senses and goes out alone again? Audience means many; could the actor call the visitor the audient? That seemed unnatural and unclear. Sometimes he thought: my visitor. Sometimes, thinking of the ordeals of education and religion, he would call the visitor the candidate. In the end, the actor would just think: the man, the woman, the child. And sometimes he would, for that brief intersection of their lives, he would think: my man, my woman, my child.

People who came out of the theater, especially when discussion with other visitors failed to find common interpretations of shared experiences, were often angry. Most people didn't try to talk about their experiences. Some seemed disappointed, some happy. No one ever seemed to ask for their money back. Out each would come, one at a time always, step down the ordinary wooden steps, look around, often with embarrassment plain in the face, and hurry to rejoin friends or family below. Then away they would drift, into the crowd, or into the ordinary dark. Ten minutes later, another would step down.

Ten minutes is a long time in the dark. What happened? What did the actor say? What stories or myths did he embody for his audience?

In early days, it would tend to be a simple story, one based on classical mythology or heroic legend, one familiar enough even to his simplest visitor—*Perseus Casts the Still-living Head of Medusa into the Sea*, or *The Boy Stumbles into the Cave in the Kyffhaeuser where The Emperor Sleeps Sword in Hand*, or *Arion the Minstrel Thrown into the Sea by Pirates Is Rescued by A Friendly and Courteous Dolphin*.

As the theater grew more successful, the actor was able to retain the services of other artists to act in his productions, as well as lay helpers who kept the wagon in good condition, and took care of the horses. However many actors and actresses might be involved, they all had to content themselves with working within the dark space of the tiny theater. Visitors now who passed through such multiple encounters might stumble out into the warm Whit Monday afternoon having been caressed and buffeted and berated in unknown tongues. However grand the actor's conceptions might become, they all had to make do with the little space, the little time, four yards, ten minutes. Words and voices crowded into the experience sometimes were remembered—who knows how many townsmen would recall, more or less vaguely, all their lives the whispered and hasty jargon of the dark?

The actor found in time what we all know, that sensation drives out words, and any texts or dialogues the audience might remember would ever be shadowy, discontinuous, a white noise behind the brilliant focus of an actual touch, or a drop of water landing on the wrist, or a feather drawn across the nape of the neck.

So husbands would rarely like the way their wives looked when they stepped down the rickety steps of the wagon. More than once the theater had to pack up quickly and move on. Complaints and accusations were made: insinuations and seductions, wrongful touching, all the usual business of the dark. None of that was true to the actor's intention. A touch never meant an arrangement between people, not for him. For him, a touch was pure leaving, a gesture in which everything here went there, and never came back. A touch was all giving.

But the police were bothersome at times. Once, in Metz, an examining magistrate had revealed himself as both learned in theatrical history, and sympathetic to the bohemian life of theater folk; nonetheless, he could not grasp the strange turn-about the actor had contrived: many actors working a single member of the audience. The magistrate indicated clearly that what was good enough for Euripides and Corneille was good enough for our own people: it is well for people in the mass to be edified in the mass. The actor's innovations might be regarded as a menace to society, inasmuch as it withdrew an individual from the mass, and a society can endure only a limited number of individuals at any one time. The actor took the hint, and hurried to leave the region.

Time was finally more oppressive than policemen. The actor grew old, as one does, and lost his taste for the overlapping unseen dance of the many around the one. Gradually he let the other actors go, and kept only one servant who cooked and took care of the equipment. He was allowed to beat the big bass drum that had come to replace the actor's mandolin as a signal to the crowd. But the servant was never allowed to perform in the theater.

It had come back to the way it began—the actor alone in the dark, waiting for someone to talk to, someone to touch. Changing the space around them, making them hear. Making them feel. Sometimes, as he got older, he felt that all the speeches of all the plays he had ever performed in his early days, not just his own roles but all the language of which the roles were part, all that language had flowed into him, and flowed out now through the least gesture of his fingers, the least whisper of his breath. Sound of his breath. Touch of his hand.

One night he realized that through all the performances of that very hot evening, he had spoken no single actual word. And then he knew that language did not need speech to come into the world; language passed through him to them, and it did not matter if he said nothing they could hear or remember. Nothing they could misquote. Nothing they could forget.

And when that wordlessness had come, the actor felt that at last he had entered into the real play, the single drama he really meant all along. Each person who came into the theater was different, and each received the actor's play directly, unconfused by words, undefiled by story. It happened to them, and that's what the theater was, something happening to them.

4

Old men seek the sun, and he was no exception. No longer did he perform in the rainy north; little by little moved down the Italian peninsula, happy to be warm, happy to be listened to. Old he was, and perhaps not too strong, but strong enough to perform every night. He liked little towns best, places he had not known about before, places not mentioned on the old maps he had been carrying half a century, carefully marking the venues of his performances. Eventually he reached Calabria, the toe of the boot, and was disappointed to find rocky uplands and harsh weather. Everyone told him that Sicily was the place for him, sunny Sicily, dreaming its memories of Greeks and Africans and Carthaginians and Normans. All that sounded fine to him, but how was he to get his theater across to the great island?

At last he thought: perhaps really I am the theater. Maybe I do not need a box on wheels, horses, drums. Maybe I don't even need the dark. I will go and see for myself. Maybe I am enough. Maybe I am enough.

So he took passage on a little ferry and crossed to Sicily, and wandered alone from town to town, with nothing but a mule he'd bought to carry his gear and sometimes, when he was tired, to carry him.

He would come to a town and stand in the marketplace or public square and hold up a piece of cloth that said that the theater was with them, and that performances would begin at such and such a time in such and such a place. And at the designated hour he would stand there, and solemnly lead, always one by one, each member of the audience into a patch of ground he had marked out, scratching a boundary in the earth with the stick he leaned on when walking. And in that bounded space he would perform what he could of the theater.

It was hard for him, and he really didn't know, couldn't tell, if his performances were working. Maybe a long time ago he had lost any idea of successful or unsuccessful, availing or unavailing. More and more, the theater just was, just happened to people the way weather happened to them. Is weather successful, he asked himself?

One evening, when the sun had not yet stopped gilding the ruddy tile roof of the church, a woman came forward to him from the audience. She was taller than most, and struck him as curiously familiar. He took her by the arm to lead her into the enclosure, and was startled to find her sleeve soaking wet. The whole woman was drenched, and cool water seemed to flow from her. His own arm was wet now from touching her, but he did not let her go. He remembered from long ago the story of the woman who had lain in the fountain. That was in Sicily. It must be the same woman. Maybe in every age there is a Sicily, a woman from the fountain come to touch him. Was it she?

It was she, yes it was. But this woman was young, and he was very old. How had she stayed young such a long time, while he had spent so much of his life trying to understand, trying to learn how to make people feel the way she felt? Had he been born old? Was he always old? She was young and he was old, and she was smiling at him.

She said again, "Yes, I am the woman to whom the hawk came down. I am the one it happened to. I am the one to whom things happen. You are the man who makes things happen to people. Who are you?"

That was not a nice question to ask him. He had brought so much to so many places, places where pale listless folk lived, places in ancient Alpine valleys where the names of flowers sounded like people coughing, places by the Black Sea where no two people in the audience were of the same race, he had been everywhere. He had touched so many people. He had outlived his horses, his traveling theater, outlived even the words of his play. He had just touched them, so many people. So many! And this girl, really just a girl, asked him who he was!

The man thought that maybe he had turned into god, some kind of god, but whatever he was, he was very old. And tired, tired and hot. He held her hands and pulled her down with him as he knelt down, then lay down on the ground. He lay beside the woman, and without even asking permission, put his head in her lap.

Her wet hands lay on his forehead a while. When he looked at her, he had to squint against the strong setting sun to see her face. She was smiling, even though he had not answered her question. He lay for a space of time, then in a little while he rolled over and burrowed, pressing his face into her lap. She gently pulled up her skirt to make this easy for him. His body relaxed, so that he lay with his head resting across her thighs, his face turned downward. He licked softly and timidly, his tongue rough along the soft inner thigh. He did this tentatively, the way an animal or bird picks cautiously at some unfamiliar thing to see if it is his food. He must have liked what he tasted, for he licked again. But by then he had passed at last beyond thinking. And before the little wet lick had dried on her skin, he was gone from the world.

II

The Wandering Jew

BY NOW I HAVE FORGOTTEN whatever it was I am supposed to have done. A crime maybe, or an incivility
on a public street. In those days I must have imagined
that an action had no consequences. I know that a stone
dropped into a pool makes ripples, but I also know the
ripples stop when they reach the side of the pond. I did
not know that the world is a body of water that has no
rim. We shiver in endlessness, and an act has no end.

I guess it was a small thing, since I feel no pain, no
wheels of Ixion or sneering headwaiters of Tantalus. What
was it? We were all Jews together, and one of them became
famous, and this is the one I am supposed to have said or
done something to. I remember his eyes, half weary, half
something else, like a man with his mind on other things,
as he looked towards me and said something about waiting for him.

Maybe he wasn't even looking at me. I don't remember having done anything to him, I mean I really can't look into myself and find a small guilty feeling mousing around furtively in the granary of my heart. Maybe I did nothing at all. Maybe he was really talking to the loudmouth next to me who was yelling in bad Greek. Maybe he was talking to the pretty woman in front of me who was crying, but whose soft hips pressed back against me. Maybe he was talking to us all. Whatever, whoever, I heard his words. A fate belongs to the one who hears it spoken. I heard it, and it became mine. I wander, tired myself now, almost but not quite tired of myself, my mind hard put to it to stick to one thing. I feel now the way he looked then, and I wonder when he will come again or I will go.

Andromeda

ANDROMEDA IS IN THE ROOM. Andromeda is chained to the radiator. When the heat comes on she tends to struggle to keep from making contact. When it is cold she lets herself slump against its shapely iron fins. When she is weary sometimes she sinks down. Standing up or crouching down are her choices. Except when the metal's neither hot nor cold, then she arches back on the radiator and lies there as well as she can.

> *This is a story from Greek mythology — a lovely ailment of the mind that is still very much alive.*

What is the nature of the monster who comes to molest or devour her?

When she stands there against the iron, she has only a very few choices. For example, when the time is right

> *Things, it is things that eat us up, one after another, we are never free from the bite of them. But things are not the only things.*

for her to rest against the radiator, she can lean back in such a way that the cleft between her buttocks lines up with one of the clefts between the fins of the radiator. Alternatively, she can rest against the radiator in such a way her cleft is visited by one of the fins. In the case of (One), left and right buttock are dug into close to the cleft. In the case of (Two), the metal presses further out along each cheek while the penetrant iron fin presses in. Little as the difference is, she can feel it. So she has a choice between one sensation and another.

Of such choices are human lives made.

The chain around her waist is long enough to let her move her body away from the radiator, but not long enough for her to lie down. She can slump or stand, or, in milder seasons, actually perch on the radiator, awkwardly, to be sure, but sustained, sustained by what imprisons her. Her hands are free, though.

And what will she do with her free hands?

One thing is that whenever anybody comes through the door or even just looks into the room, she deftly opens her blouse and shows her breasts to whoever it is that comes in, in case it happens to be Perseus. She has never met Perseus, but has heard a lot about him, and a voice (the kind we mean when we say 'at the back of my mind') inside tells her that Perseus is the one who will set her free.

She doesn't even know if Perseus is a man or a woman, a child or an animal. The name sounds masculine, grammatically, but grammar has never been her strong suit. Grammar belongs to moving around the world and discovering where things are, and how they connect with one another, in front, behind, to this side, over there, on the other side of the mountain. Grammar is all about where things are with respect to one another, and Andromeda is only here. So she doesn't really know what Perseus will be like.

"Would you like to see my breasts?" she asks everyone who comes into the room.

Is anyone free? The question is absurd, the answer tragic.

"Suit yourself," one might say. Or another might say, "I am pledged to someone else, please don't." Or a third might answer, "Do not trouble yourself on my account, I have seen enough breasts to last me," or "I have breasts of my own."

She did not know what Perseus would look like. She knew the name meant: the one who destroys. She thinks about that. We should think about it too. So when he comes through the door slamming and shrieking and swinging his sledgehammer his scramasax his evil image his flashlight his rifle, we can calm ourselves like rabbis soothing the anxiety of exile with intricate unanswerable questions. Isn't it strange that he destroys. Why doesn't he just come in with clippers or scissors, just like a sunbeam in October, or with a coarse steel file, come in and cut her loose and run away with her?

Her nature is to be bound. His nature is to destroy. This is what we must conclude. And again, it is our nature to come to such conclusions.

All encounters in real time perplex both the savior and the saved. One day at last the real Perseus comes through the door. It is Perseus, it really is. He comes in. It is his nature to come in. Andromeda looks at him with neither hope nor fear. She is entirely engaged in being bound. She needs only to know if he is a part of her story. So she asks him her question.

"Would you like to see my breasts? I would like to show them to you."

She speaks gently. Her voice is deep and just a liitle harsh, the way brooks can sound when they run too quickly over jagged rocks in spring.

His actual desires	"Very much," he says, "yes, but it is not so much that I want to see them, but that I want you to want to show them to me—for your own reasons."

He speaks no more and no less than the truth.

It seems he wants to be fair, to let her know his investment in the situation. Desire is always an investment. Even if it is a desire he never even knew existed until, with her words, he was offered its fulfilment. Then his heart, is that what it is, his heart filled with yearning to see her very breasts. What does it mean about us that the eyes can so feed the heart by acts of desperate looking? He wants to see.

He never means to sound scornful or cool. Yes was what he means, yes is what he says. He wants to see her breasts, and says so. Yes means yes. No wonder they call him The Destroyer.

Meantime she has unbuttoned the big white buttons on her black rayon blouse. She spreads the blouse open, a priest revealing the mysteries. Perseus kneels down in front of her, he knows what to do, her breasts are at the level of his face, he leans forward and presses his face against her breasts, full and warm they are, and he realizes he can see them better with his eyes closed. The eyes are only a special place of skin, he thinks, and licks the smooth of the breast where it levels off to the plain of the chest, then slips his tongue down along until it works itself between the skin of the chest and the skin of the full breast, the warm soft fragrant place. Between skin and skin.

He wonders: why do we do this? Is my sensation my sensation? Or is it just an excitement that pleases me, an excitement that is just my cognitive response to a genuine sensation that she feels, a sensation she knows how to telepath to me? Is all my pleasure just giving pleasure? Don't I feel anything myself?

He tries to feel. But Andromeda can't move, can only be moved. And Perseus can't be moved, just move. What a dumb world, and yet such beautiful words there are in it!

Which of all those words will free her? He has no tools with him to cut chains or break radiators. What can a hand do, or a tongue? A word might do it, if he can find the word. She waits for him to know it and say it. She is good at waiting. We hope he is good at finding. At saying.

Offshore

———————————◆———————————

CAUGHT AS WE WERE between the outgoing tide and the crush of logs thrust into the estuary by the last push of the Matanga, I had no recourse but to close my eyes and pray to Pollux: "Come with your brother / To my bad boat," I prayed in my Saxon. And before you knew it, a swell of contradictory currents lifted my hull onto a Sand Bar, and there we determined to wait till the Rising Tide would—we surmised—painlessly lift us loose, and we could make Land. Sure enough, the sky filled with a peculiar violet light just then, a characteristic of the presence of gods, or else of a typhoon coming.

O weather may be, all of them no doubt are, gods, they all are gods, but I cleave to my own gods, The Young Men Bright over Bowsprit who had just saved us, and Bellerophon the white-faced on his white-blazed steed who treads the dappled Wave, and Free Venus, who holds us all in Her red-painted hands and sees all the way down our green eyes with her own.

My second mate, Mr Akrophron, came up beside me with a plate of fruit, last of the Blood Limes we carried from Sparagmos; we sucked content in silence, spitting seed and rind into the shallow turbulent wash beside the ship. Some of the rind, though, I chewed small and swallowed. It is rumored to have virtue against Dropsy and the Stone, afflictions I fear since I was born beneath the Claws of the Scorpion.

We stood close, he and I, our arms over each other's shoulders in the posture called Faithful Sons At Their Father's Plough. Presently he began to sing a song from his native Thessaly, whose language few Greeks—and no one else at all—can understand. Tuneful, though, with certain minorish intervals reaching upwards that affected me powerfully, as if something were trapped in my heart and kept trying to rear up and claw its way out, the way a trapped Mouse might vainly strive to scramble out of a bucket. Poor Mouse. Poor little mouse in somebody's heart. Poor little heart. Anybody's.

From the crew's quarters came the disquieting smell of Fish stewing. Several of the seamen, flushed faced fellows from the coasts of Pwent, had caught some Bream, which their religion lets them eat, and were cooking it now with mallow leaves and some shabby dried-up Parsnips, for the sweetness. Though I mislike fish of all sorts, the smell made me hungry, and I became aware I hadn't eaten solid food since midmorning. I clapped my hands, and young Irich brought me my big wooden bowl full of porridge with green onions and pickled cabbage chopped into it, and a bowl of something for Mr Akrophron.

We dined under the evening sky, and soon Mr Thorgil joined us, my First Mate, already chewing on a surprisingly meaty Ox Bone. We fell to arguing about the gods, as so often we do. Mr Thorgil stared at the water all round us, the teak trunks bobbing and clustered, heaving with the lift of waters. Here and there some of the natives were walking on the logs, deft boys who stroll from log to log as if ashore. Their business was to rope the logs together loosely into great rafts that could be floated across the Straits. This had to be done briskly, before the logs dispersed into the choppy Sea beyond the shallow, silted-up lagoon at the mouth of the Matanga, where we lay at anchor.

My mate said, in his gruff eloquent way, "Those logs, these logs, that's just how we sign or mark the gods where I arose. A tree trunk means the god. And if a man propose to come to some new strand, he carries a God Log with him on his boat, and casts it into the Sea, and follows it till it comes to the Shore—however far that may be—and where it touches land, that is his Place, his 'Stead' as we call it."

"What if it come not to land?"

"Still he must follow it. The god knows. Wood shows the way."

"And if it carries instead out into open sea?"

"You speak of my own case. That is what happened to me. Far from the Herring Isles came my log to land, a weary watch of winters bode I the battering of my boat, until the eely avenues of ocean led me late to Latinland and so to Sicel's shore I sauntered, and reared my rigid Godpole righteous there under Aetna's uneasy everlasting

Smokes. And there you found me, friend, and friends we are."

I thought that seeing so many logs bobbing this way and that all at one time through the bay might make Thorgil worry, as if he must needs obey each and every trunk, and make all their destinations his own. Not so. He explained he knew no god whose tree was Teak. Doubtless there are such Deities aplenty, but since they had not made themselves known to him, he need not bestir himself. The gods he knew, they knew linden and oak, maple and beech and mistletoe, apple and ash—enough for him, that glad variety.

"A man's a fool to look for god, my people say," he said, "a wise man lets god find him." He said no more.

Irich brought us cups of tea made from the leaves of the coffee tree that grows down Yemen way, on both shores of the Narrow Sea. I took two cups since I meant to watch, alert for the turning of the tide.

The Priest's Mistress's Story

from the Lydian

I N A YARD ON AN OLD ESTATE
a bad man tried to burn a deed of conveyance
belonging to a dead man,
a priest who had loved me,
he was my master,
he owned me, he defined me
by his kindness, I was his beloved
and he was my legal defender
against any other, another
came and tried to do me harm,
to give him this harm too, saying
"she will define a house,
she will live in it a year
as member of the commune
until her brother comes"

but I have no brother, I lived a year
with my master, he gave me
thing after thing and pressed me to him
I was devoted to him, a god,
and he was devoted to the god he worked for,
priest, divine activity, construction
of the way we feel about the world,
memory and everything
it means to be, to be here
or even be there, in the yard
where the bad man, this one, the grandson
of my mother, tried to write in
inside the document
a prescription that would surround the house
and fill in his own bad name
and make it his, he wanted it
to be complete upon completion,
to spoil what my master had defined
so broadly, to destroy, to steal, to take in hand
what my master had constructed.
I wanted to go forward with what I had,
to defend whatever was across and through
whatever is, I wanted to do and do
so everything I did would take effect.
He was a robber, he tried to take
what we possess, all that a family is
that a man and a woman make
just the two of them together and then he died,
my master, and, and only the dog
was left for me to trust,
the dog and the house and the memory of the man,
the memory of the man inside

the memory of the house, the shadow,
the dog runs through the memory of the
house he constructed, the man, the priest
who loved me, I trust him, he made
a house, he constructed it,
he abolished the shadows,
he built out of bricks, the bricks were light,
he has built a house
and made a curse against those who hurt me
or hurt his house, a priest's curse
he wrote above the door of his house
(I am his house, he is my door)
he wrote it as an inscription, he dipped
his finger in the blood of my calendar,
he wrote with my blood that this is my house
and a curse on him who would take it away,
only a man would try to take a house away,
he put the words on the house
the house was on the land,
he walked around the land with me,
our little yard inside the walls, he walked
until he discovered water, he swears
a promise to the gods, he tells me how to pray,
pray this way, he says, he lifts
a double-bladed axe above his head, like this, he says,
and swings it down on the ground
saying I am the lord, speak to me,
I am the lord of this ground, just this little yard
on earth, o earth, earth speak to me,
this tongue of mine can break a wall,
he breaks the earth and water flows, a fountain,
he sets up a column of brick beside it

he smears clay on the brick and writes in the clay,
writing is the arm of a man,
writing is the strength of his arm
that lasts in the form of a wall
against what other people mean,
a man's strength lasts in his word,
the deed of a house, he gave
the house to me, Afala the bad man
cannot take it from me,
he tries to burn the deed in the yard,
the hide won't burn, the clay
refuses to take even one word back.

A wall is a man's valor,
a man is strong a wall is strong,
there is nothing a bad man can do,
he tries for a month, he begs for the king
to do anything, the king
does nothing, the king does not love
a bad man, he says to the bad man, he says to Afala,
go to your own area, do not kill what is good,
what is good is the property of a man or a woman,
this woman, they flourish in possession
of a house, this house, the date tree is beside it,
the well is beside it, my priest found it
and gave it to her, gave her the house, gave her
the well and the waters of the well, all the water,
I am the king, I approve what he did
I approve what she has, let her live here
in the house in the town of towers, Sard, this house,
a house of a woman is a self of a man,
the woman's house I approve, I take care of her,

I send men to take care of her,
go away, bad man, I send men into her tower,
they climb to the top and they possess a column,
a column in the shape of the trunk of a tree,
a date palm, they write on the column
the same words the priest wrote, they write again
it is hers, a woman belongs to her self,
she is powerful because she recognizes evil,
she tells me the man is bad and I believe her,
the same words the priest spoke
curse the evil man, they sanctify
this house where the woman lives
with the live dog and the shade of her master
the priest, she lives with his shadow
in the house, the house is a house for the living
and a tomb for the dead, leave her
to her living, what else does she have,
it is as the elders said, it is good to build,
it is good to take wood and brick and make a house,
a house is your heir, a house inherits
everything you mean, the king says,
you will not destroy it, I eliminate you
from the ranks of those I esteem, go,
and the bad man went away
and the woman goes on living in her house
the very one the priest constructed
meaning something she tries to understand
by living in the thing he made.

*This narrative is a translation of the Lydian Concise
Dictionary in the "Indoeuropean Project" website.*

The Logic of the World

———————⟫•◉•⟪———————

EASTER WAS LONG PAST. It was the quiet time of year
when nothing was happening but the slow dawning
of grain and fruit, the green shoots thickening to stems,
stems beginning to round out towards what, months later,
in the quietest time, would be ripe for harvest. Deep earth
was asleep. Only her skin was lively, the powers and forms
she had been dreaming all winter long were off on their
own now, and she could sleep.

So that even here, where there was no sowing and no
reaping, reigned the incessant uprising of tree and fern
and toadstool, the ever-upward life of the forest itself, in
the quiet heat of afternoon. The lilies rosy-speckled like
swift river fish had faded now, but the Pentecost roses
were getting ready to blossom.

The knight cared about such things, though he didn't

know much about their names. He noticed, though, and cared about the thickening, the coming of color into the plant, lifting some pale or vivid hue magically right out of the green, how did it happen, how could the brown twig and green leaf suddenly start to yield scarlet, yellow, or the rare of blue? Where do colors come from? He remembered, though he couldn't see it right now, the way sometimes the moisture caught in his eyelashes caught the sun so that tiny rainbows formed and scattered. What are colors?

He let himself think about such things. It was good to have a keen eye, to keep his vision whetted by noticing the slight difference between today and tomorrow, as the plant shows it, so subtly but so clearly, by its changes. Keep vision whetted by noticing the patterns that insects make in the air, or how certain tamped down foliage means a deer has slept here with her fawn. He was good at watching.

And on the old track through the dark woods there was much to watch, evidence of people before him come and gone, and others whose presence, neither friendly nor hostile, he could feel nearby, unseen, ever-present. They were people who did not concern themselves with travelers; a knight like himself, a monk or two, or even a company of pilgrims, they just amounted to weather in the woods, passing, not really there.

The knight felt almost comforted by their presence, at peace with their indifference. Just as he felt indifferent but alert to the trees and herbs he passed by, or slept beneath, or nibbled in the morning, when he knew this leaf was safe, to wake his breath and shape the waking air.

It was still morning as he rode, and he was beginning to feel the first stirrings of hunger. He had plenty of bread in his saddlebag, and sweet water in his leather bottle, but he was a well-reared young man, and knew that one should not eat while doing some other thing, in this case riding, watching, understanding the world he passed through. Eating takes the soul inside, to survey the food's journey to the center – that is how he had been taught. And taught too that doing things while eating sapped the nourishment from the food, and also drained the soul from the other thing he might be doing. He had seen other people, some of them knights or priests even, munching while they walked or worked wood or read in a book—he shook his head to think of such folly, that people should live on the earth and not understand the simplest things about their bodies' relations with the place they lived in.

The track he followed was narrow but clear. He rode cautiously, frequently having to duck beneath a heavy branch, or gently lift a younger one aside—do not break the tree that shelters the path, that was another thing he knew.

Just ahead now he could see, far up ahead, in something of a clearing where more sun came through, another traveler on the path. He was seated on a fallen log, it seemed, and the knight could see a big bag slumped beside the man. As the knight drew closer, he could see that the seated man was a leper, his walking staff with rattle-top lying beside him, his shabby old tunic still showing clear enough the huge rough heart-shape painted on it in rust. The leper was eating, but dropped his loaf and went to pick up the staff and rattle it, courteously, to warn the knight.

"Good morning, Sir Leper," the knight called out in a friendly way. The leper let the staff fall, and smiled up. His face was mostly still there, and the smile was easy enough to look at.

"Good morning, Lord Knight," the leper replied, each man courteously elevating the social status of the other. Perhaps the leper had been a man of better station once upon a time.

There was not much to say. But the knight lingered, of a mind to share and inquire.

"Have you food enough, Sir Leper? I have a bit in my satchel."

"Thank you kindly, my lord, but I have some meat in mine too. And there is good water in a spring a little way beyond, you'll pass it in five minutes, if you need. It breaks out of a single rock upright among cool ferns, I like the place, but do not linger there, because I am as you see me."

The knight knew no easy way to respond to that, and turned his words aside.

"What is this place we're in? Whose forest is this?"

"I don't know its name, or it may not have one, and I have lived near at hand most of my life, apart from the years I wandered in the Holy Land that taught me to wear such clothes as these," said the leper, sweeping one hand down along his tunic blazoned with the Heart of Pity, as they called it, that all lepers in this land must wear. "They say the woods are owned by the Abbey of Saint Ulfric. but no one lives in that abbey any longer, and the last abbot died when I was a child. Whoever may own the land, there is no doubt who controls it. For this whole forest is in the clutches of a Dragon who lives in a gorge only a mile or a mile and a half, depending on what path you take to reach it, from where we are sitting."

"A dragon!" exclaimed the knight. "Does he do great mischief in the woods?"

"Not to the trees, but you will have noticed, perhaps, that no animals have crossed your path, and few are the birds that flew over you."

"I had not noticed. Why is that?"

"Most have been consumed by the Dragon," said the leper. "My uncleanness must spoil his appetite, since he has never bothered me, though I have seen him half a dozen times, and I am sure he's seen me more often that that, since little does he miss in what goes forward."

"What does he look like, when you see him, this dragon?"

"Much as you suppose. Vast and sinuous and mostly green, with flakes of bony stuff atop his spine that would slice a man in half. Wings he has as well, of a pale bluish color, translucent like the wings of a bat, and very long. His face is an interesting one: he has the fangs you'd expect, but set in a muzzle of some nobility, more lion than snake, more eagle than lion. Hard to be sure, since his face seems to change its bones with his mood."

"That is very odd," said the knight. He was silent for a while, thinking of what he had heard. Then asked:

"If the dragon has eaten up all the deer and boar and hares in these woods, what does he live on, do you think?"

"I know the answer to that," said the leper. "He leaves the woods and raids the towns and granges all about, on the far side of the forest, away from the side from which you came. He is a plague and a bother to them, but strange to say, though he breathes fire like any dragon, he never burns down a house or croft or mill. Mostly he'll seize cattle or sheep, a goat or a dog, and that will sate him. But sometimes he has been known to snatch a maiden, wrap her in his coils and fly away with her to his gorge. At least that is what people think. The bones of the girls are never found."

"That is a sad and shameful thing, that a young woman be carried off at all, let alone by such a beast."

"Beast he may be, though I'm not sure of that, since I have heard him talk."

"Talk!"

"Yes, and not the way crows talk, for example, where you have to hold your heart and mind a certain way to understand what they're saying. No, this dragon talks as you and I are talking now, using words, most of which I recognize."

"Have you spoken with him, then?" asked the knight, a little doubtful all at once of the character of this leper.

"Never, but I have heard him speaking. Whether to himself or to another I could not tell. Out of fear I kept my distance. Damaged and distressed as it is, this body is still precious to me, and I would fain keep it a while longer."

"What does he say, this dragon? What is there for him to speak about, I wonder."

The leper closed his eye and thought a bit before he answered.

"You know, lord, I am not sure. While he was speaking, I understood perfectly what he said and what he meant. But afterwards, and now, all I could do was remember understanding. But what I understood, that I can't remember."

"It seems to me," said the knight, "that I should go and

see what this dragon has to say for himself. And if he does not give a good account, I suppose I must seek with God's help to slay him, and rid the forest and the farms of his harm. This seems then to be an adventure that has come to me. Thank you, Sir Leper."

"That is gracious of you, Lord Knight, but better to thank me later, when you see whether or not this is a good thing you undertake."

'How could it, with God's help, fail to be good?"

"I could not say, Lord Knight, but the dragon may not be of a mind to be slain. Or he may speak with such wiles as to dissuade you. Or even win you to his cause, whatever that might be."

"Speaking of that, you speak well, Sir Leper, if I may say so. Your words are intelligent and suave and well-chosen, dare I say it, and much wittier than mine. You remind me of certain clerics who had the kindness to instruct me when I was very young."

"Yes, Lord Knight, I was a priest once upon a time, and went with the Jerusalem Farers on their crusades, to give them counsel and keep them honest along the way, much good it did."

A leper priest is a scary thing indeed, the young knight thought, but wasn't sure why it should be so. Why scarier than a leper farmer or a leper soldier? Yet it was, almost as if it meant that something was wrong in the way the world was made. That a priest should give up woman and begetting and owning and amassing, and yet be subject to this degrading disease. And all a priest's learning went for naught. Not naught, though, since here he was being instructed by this wise priest.

"I grieve for your distress," said the knight, and the other knew he meant not just the leprosy but also his sadness at the human condition, where rutting soldiers would not listen to their priests, and stole and spoiled and ravened.

"Bless you for your understanding," said the leper, and said no more.

The knight sat a while longer and thought about what he had learned. Now it is a knight's business to balance the iniquity in the moral world and the imperfections in the natural order with his own virtue and prowess and that special quality of responsible loving-kindness called honesty. It would appear, and so it seemed to him, that the activities of the dragon, as reported, constituted an imperfection in this forest in particular, and the scheme of things in general, one that should be mended. And the code of Holy Adventure, by which knights have always lived, and still do live, calls for the knight who discovers the flaw in the pattern to be the one who heals it.

The leper was sitting quietly, and the knight supposed the man wanted to get on with his meal – the sun was straight overhead now. But the leper made no gesture one way or another, just sat.

"Sir Leper," asked the knight, "could you show me the way to the dragon's gorge?"

The leper smiled, and gently thrust his rear leg forward. Only now did the knight see that there was scarcely a foot at the end of the leg, just a mass of clotted cloths tied round a stump it did not bear to think about.

"My lord will see that I am not skilled at walking, these days, and will forgive me for not keeping him company. I walk little as I can, and on the softest places, where the pine needles let fall the soft, safe road that is my bed as well. I will tell you, though, how to meet your dragon."

How strange, the knight thought, that the priest had already made the dragon the knight's own.

"From this place keep onward as you were going. As I said before, you will soon come to a spring among the ferns—it will be on your right side as you go. Pause and drink—the water is healthy and bracing. Just past the spring you will see, on the same side, a thickety place, all rustling aspen leaves and shadow. In the thicket you will soon find, God willing, a little path, evident, wide enough for your horse I think. Take this and follow it. It rises slowly through trees to a bare hill, climbs the hill—it is no more than a mile from the spring—and from the top, you will look down into the gorge of the one of whom we have spoken. God be with you, Lord Knight."

"And with you, Sir Priest, and thank you."

The knight made a civil gesture, which was returned. Then he urged his horse onward. In a few minutes man and rider came to the rock among ferns. The knight dismounted and drank, and drank again. And felt again the hunger he'd been feeling before the leper. Why not eat his midday meal here?

He did so. And as he chewed on the good grainy bread, he thought a little about priest and dragon, maiden and duty, then drew his mind back to the bread. Because thinking about things while eating is no better than riding or plowing a field while eating. Eat while eating, ride while riding, sleep while sleeping. But thinking has a way of creeping in, the way dream creeps into blameless sleep and tells its incoherent stories. Not easy not to think. Best to think about bread, his jaws chewing, his body dark with waiting.

When he swallowed as much of his bread as he'd let

himself eat this summery day with supper far away, he packed up his things, drank again from the spring, and remounted. Soon enough he spied a little track off through the aspens, and veered off that way, hoping it was the right one. A dark way indeed, and the leaves on their slender branches had a way of being mobile, moving before him, beside him, behind him, as if they were opening the curtain of themselves and leading him further in.

Now that the leper had alerted him to the absence of beast and fowl, the knight kept an ear open for any bird cry he might hear. It was true, the forest was quiet, very quiet, apart from the noises he made brushing through the trees. A few times there did come the clear call of a crow from up ahead, a sound he liked hearing. It made him easier about his choice of path. He trusted crows, and any place where they gathered.

A mile or so the leper priest had said. Ambling though the horse was, and the leaves thick around them, he expected they'd find himself at the hill in no great while, and indeed the ground was gradually, perceptibly rising before him. Soon the aspens gave way to a treeless slope close-covered with heather, and he spurred his horse up. Again the crows called ahead of him, more than one —three, he guessed, from the timbres of their cry. At the top of what seemed not a hill but a ridge, the knight looked down into the gorge he expected to see.

Deep it was, and running arrow-straight from south to north (it seemed) through the forest. Seventy or eighty feet down, a feeble stream winked along the narrow valley. On the far side of the gorge, tall pines stood, and two or three crows seemed tossed from branch to branch, but no longer did they cry. He had come, he thought, to where he was supposed to be, so no more directions were needed. Here it is. The steep slopes of the gorge fell away—walking back and forth along the rim, he could spy no trail, and the slope was too steep for any horse. Where was the dragon?

The slope in front of him was densely matted with juniper and cedar and heather, while the slope on the far side seemed crusted with a low, thick ground cover, a row of spiky bushes running along it halfway down. What he saw was quiet, and gave him no sense of awe or fear. As a good and honest knight, he knew fear, knew it well, and knew how to deal with it, most times. Without fear there could be no courage—his teachers had taught him that. Without fear there can only be a creeping uneasiness, a draining, enervating malaise. Fear is brilliant, though, and summons even cowards to be brave. These were good thoughts to be having, he thought, when looking for dragons. But where was the dragon? No smell, no sound, no glimpse of his presence. Or of what he might have done. In earlier encounters with dragons he had heard about, the knight had always found near the caverns scattered bones, garments stripped from poor travelers devoured, bracelets, pieces of gold, even, though most of those were buried deep within some cave or burrow. The knight looked for such evidence now, and found nothing. Was this the right place? He wondered about the leper, whether a man like that, however well-spoken and kindly-acting, might not have, in his own despair, come to take pleasure in leading other men astray, as once he had tried vainly to lead them towards the good. Where was the dragon?

The knight slipped off his horse, tethered the creature to a sturdy thick old juniper bush and plucked off a few of those cloudy blue berries. He mashed them in his fingers, inhaled the heady smell of them, they smelled like a rain-shower on a hot sunny day. He dropped the seedy pulp, but licked his fingers. The taste was nothing at all like the smell. That is how things are. The knight sat down cross-legged, and waited, staring down into the ravine.

It was pleasant being where he was. The horse found nourishment in deep unvisited grasses among the shrubs. A quiet wind was moving, and it dawned on the knight that it was because the wind was coming from over his shoulders that he smelled none of the stench people had told him to expect anywhere that dragons had stayed a while.

He wondered what manner of dragon this might be. The description the priest had given could, depending on just how faithful a describer he had been, suit several sorts of dragon: the Cloud Worm (and the blue wings suggested it) who nests in earth but spends most of his day aloft; or the Diggon Nail, who burrows straight down in the earth and (it seems an evil miracle) turns himself inside out to shoot out again, arrow-swift, from the earth to seize its prey; or the Riverlord, who lived mostly in streams and lakes to keep his fires banked against the moment of need. But the nobility the priest had noted in the dragon's face, 'more lion than snake, more eagle than lion', did not match any of those three kinds. None of the other dragons he knew about had wings at all, or tall scales on their back-bones. So he would await the encounter, and learn.

As he sat there, reviewing his knowledge of such mat-ters as might be useful to recall in the next while, he grew sleepy. He knew well enough that sleep is not to be fought off—only enemies are to be fought, but not to be indulged either—only bad friends need to be indulged.

No, sleep was a good friend, and should be met candidly, and only when the time was right. The time seemed right, nothing asked itself of him, he let his eyelids close and let himself drift towards sleep.

A breath of air tickled along his neck, and his eyes opened. And before he let them close again he noticed, or thought he noticed, that there was some subtle difference in the slope on the far side of the ravine. It had changed, its contour was not what it had been, but the knight could not tell just how. He decided to experiment: he closed his eyes, drifted almost away, then quickly opened them. Yes, there was a change, the curve of the bushes was different.

Then, as he watched, eyes wide, the change happened —a ripple ran through the shrubs and grasses over there, and then a stronger one. He could feel no wind to account for it, or for the next even heftier ripple. Then the whole hillside lifted up and looked at him.

For it was the dragon himself, stretched out and likely asleep, that he had been watching all this while, the tough green scales and hairy interweaves of the great body now clearly discernible, the huge head (he had thought it a distant tree) now reared halfway up the sky turned round to gaze at the knight, who felt awe and fear, states of feeling he had been trained to turn into thinking. He thought, calmly and quickly, taking and holding and releasing his breaths in the rhythm he had been taught by a monk when he was still in the hands of his master.

The dragon's head swung nearer, balancing gently halfway across the gorge. The eyes of this dragon, which was in fact the first of any kind that the knight had seen with his own eyes, these eyes that looked at him were many-colored. They did not glitter like the eyes of a snake or glisten like those of a frog. They were more cat-like, he thought, in that they seemed to go very deep into themselves and open up in there onto some other space. The hall in an ancient castle they all are coming from, he thought.

Smoke drifted out of the dragon's nostrils. Watching the smoke curl away into emptiness made him feel strange, so he concentrated on his breathing, and on letting his eyes do their work with the eyes of the animal.

Though it didn't much look like an animal.

"Can you with all your seeing see who I am?" asked the dragon. The voice was smaller than you'd imagine, deep enough, but seeming to come from nowhere. In fact, the knight looked around to see if someone else had spoken.

"No," said the dragon, "it is I who spoke. Do you feel fit to answer my question? Can you see who I am?"

"Truth to tell, I can't. I have been looking, maybe even staring, forgive me, I know that isn't polite, but somehow I imagined an animal would not mind being stared at. I mean, animals, cats for instance, or deer, or owls, are always staring."

"That is logical, Sir Parsival. But animals do mind being stared at as if they were not worth any other mode of discourse. Seeing can be very distancing. The object you look at so intently can be rendered into a mere thing by your beholding. Instead, you should try to use all of your senses, mental senses at least, to observe."

"How do you know my name?"

"I know all the names, Sir Parsival. And I know which name belongs to whom, and what everybody's real name is."

But Parsival doubted suddenly. In his mind's eye he could see the leper hobbling through the aspen grove, hurrying along a short-cut to the dragon's lair, and whispering to the dragon the name of his soon-to-be assailant. And once the knight started thinking that way, he soon imagined that the leper had deliberately lured him, for no decent reason, into this encounter with the dragon. The leper was some sort of agent or tool of the dragon. No wonder he stank and had scaly skin. But the knight didn't blurt out all of that, of course, but only said, suspiciously enough:

"I think the leper came secretly to you and told you my name."

And even as he said so, he realized that he had not told the leper his name.

"Not so, Sir Parsival, I would not need a priest to tell me what I can read from your heart."

"How did you know the leper was a priest? He wears no sign of his former glory."

"I know what everybody is, and everybody was, and some part of what everybody will be — but not all," explained the dragon, "so do not ask much about what is to come. What is to come is written in what has been. You think I am a monster (you haven't said so, but I can tell), whereas I think I myself am nothing but the logic of the world."

The dragon paused, more as if to reflect than to give the knight chance to speak, then went on:

"And the logic of the world is frightening enough, God knows."

"You dare to speak of God!"

"Everybody talks about God. Be closer!"

At that command, abruptly spoken, Parsival drew back, and his hand began to coax his sword out of its scabbard.

Yet suddenly he was closer, much closer, right in front of the dragon's face, but he had not moved. The great head had swung further towards him. He could feel the warmth of the dragon's breath on his face. He had been holding his breath, fear of the evil smell of that breath, and perhaps a righteous fear of inhaling evil itself into his innocent body. But he had to breathe, and snatched a quick inhalation. To his surprise, the smell was far from unpleasant. It reminded him of many things, the skin beside his mother's earlobe when he had kissed her goodbye, a birch-bark box he had once opened and found it full of old rose petals, most of their color gone but still a rosy scent was left for him.

"See," said the dragon, "you are beginning to stare with other senses now."

Bravely, the knight inhaled deeply. And to those other fragrances now he found others mingling too, more enigmatic, sun on hot slate, a cucumber stung by a wasp and turned a little brown around the bite, a door slammed by the wind and the dust on the threshold whirled up by its motion, tickle in the nostrils, could moonlight have a smell? And wasn't that the smell of the place in the woods where he'd seen a stag rubbing itself against a beech tree? He sneezed.

Instantly the huge membranous wings of the dragon whirled and came to rest a few feet above the knight's head.

"Why? What?" gasped the knight.

"I am shielding you from the noontime, the sun is greedy for the part of a man's soul that flies out when he sneezes and looks around and soon comes back unless it's snatched by some power. I shield you from that power."

"Thank you," said the knight, still a little breathless from his big sneeze.

"That is the first word or sign of courtesy you have shown me, Sir Parsival. Thank you for it, though some day you'll grasp that it does you more good than it does me. Now tell me, why have you come to slay me?"

"Not easy to explain, now that you ask me. At this moment, I don't feel very much like killing you. Or anything else."

"Those words are good to hear. (Even better that you speak them.) But before this very moment on the porches of my house, in pleasant sunlight, and no birds shouting, why did you think to come slay me?"

"I suppose I didn't 'think to' slay you. I really didn't think at all. I have been raised in a tradition that tells me that virtue lies in smiting or slaying the enemy. The same tradition recognizes enemies of all kinds – wolves and bears, snakes and spiders, foreigners and bandits, demons, bad neighbors, dragons, monsters, devils, and the Devil himself. All of them are against us, and we must be quick to flee them or slay them, whichever is in our power. And many of the great older brethren in my Company have distinguished themselves by slaying dragons. Or so it is said. I have never seen it done. To be truthful, you are the first dragon I have ever seen."

The dragon's head drew even closer, and turned slowly from side to side as if to give the knight a chance to see him whole. Poised now a foot or two above, the dragon spoke.

"Do I seem to you to belong to the class of enemies you have listed? Is it enough just for me to be a dragon to make you slay me, or must I first be guilty of bad behavior? And if so, what wrong have I done you?"

The knight edged back a little, to get some distance from that all-too-observant face, the broad nostrils carved in the shapely muzzle, the all-color eyes resting, always resting, calmly on him.

"No wrong, Sir Dragon. But the leper told me of your depredations on the farmlands and houses outside the woods, and the maidens you have carried off. It seemed from what he said that you were behaving exactly as dragons are said to behave. Therefore it fell to me to remedy the evil—the one who learns about it must do something about it, that is the rule."

"A good rule," said the dragon. "But what it means to 'do something,' ah, that's another matter. We should one day have a talk about that."

"Do you deny that you have raided and ravened in the plains round about?"

"Come into my house, deeper, sir, and you will find no plunder. There are no maidens here."

"Did the leper lie?"

"Perhaps the priest in him made him do it. They are creatures of books and ceremonies, priests. He, like you, has learned how dragons make nuisances of themselves, and, like you, assumes that since I am a dragon, I have done what the dragons in his books are said to do."

"So I should not be afraid of you?"

"You have done very well so far in hiding your fear, or perhaps distracting us both from it. But on the contrary, you should be very afraid of me. I told you that I am logical. Now I tell you that I am wise. The two flanks of the mind are deployed, and there is no room for stupidity or hatred or indifference. And not much room for love—just enough to keep the world at work."

"But how can I slay wisdom?"

The dragon looked very sad a moment, unless the knight deceived himself by interpreting a certain wetness of the eye.

"Slay wisdom? The priests do it all day long, and what they leave still breathing the schoolmasters and the merchants soon make away with. Wisdom, being eternal, is the easiest thing to slay."

"That's too deep for me," said the knight. And he stood up, tugging the sword loose at last from the sheath. The dragon did not move.

"O little one, o little knight, my little son! Don't you know you have already slain me? Don't you know that you'll come back tomorrow morning and there will be no dragon here, just an empty gorge, with a trickle of reddish water in it, rusty from the iron sills in this old rock. No dragon, no hoard, no maiden. But your mind will be different. You will listen to me in your head again. You will realize that, just like the cowardly creature your traditions claim I am, I have rushed into hiding. You will slowly realize that I have hidden myself in the snuggest cavern of all, deep inside your mind, and that you will never altogether silence me. Because once you have slain someone or something, you take into yourself everything they are and know and do."

Parsival did not raise his sword, but let it fall. He began to cry, wisdom is so cruel, so tender, what can he do but cry. He is young, after all, not yet seventeen, and his mother is dead.

He blinks tears out of his eyes and says "I'm sorry, I'm sorry, I meant no harm."

"And none was done," said the voice of the dragon.

"What shall I do?"

"Do what you have done. Be quick to listen, slow to lift the sword. Learn from everything you see and everyone you meet. Even lepers. Even priests. Even me."

Then there was no dragon. The air was just the same, the gorge was as it had been before; perhaps the far slope was a little more barren, perhaps not. Memory is not reliable.

The knight stowed away his sword, untethered his horse, mounted and went back down the way he had come. He wiped his eyes on his sleeve. Perhaps he should seek out the leper and disabuse of him of his false ideas about the dragon. And yet, he thought, it was those wrong ideas that had brought him to this meeting. The meeting seemed important, very important, but Sir Parsival could not exactly say how or why. He left it to work itself out in his mind, the ways things do. No need to bother the poor leper, let him think as he pleased.

Then Parsival attended to his path, the calm demeanor of his horse. Strange, he thought it, now that he thought about it, that his horse had not shied from the dragon, had not even whinnied or shifted. All through the conversation, the horse had gone on browsing. He began to think about the horse, what it must have felt. What it must know.

The Sacred Garden

O NCE A GROUP of young monks decided they must learn something hard-edged about this world people were always accusing them of running away from.

So they marked off a small plot of land behind their monastery. Not big. Maybe thirty feet by thirty feet of ordinary ground—they still thought in inches ounces and feet.

They shoved in a stake at each corner, and ran a white string from stake to stake, delimiting the space for the eye, but leaving it open to the air, light, wind, and whatever walked or flew under or over the string.

That's it. This was the origin of one of the most important experiments in the history of science. They decided they would see what would happen if they left it alone.

What will the earth do if we leave it alone? That was their

question, and they proposed to answer it not by theory but by intense reverent and sustained observation.

All day from light to dark a rota of monks took turns at watching the square that had been marked out. Never were they to enter it, not for any reason. Every evening the observing monk wrote up a log of what he had seen —mentioning all the plants in flower or in fall, all the creatures he had observed entering, leaving, flying over, browsing, resting, singing—whatever creatures took it in mind to do by themselves.

What will it do with itself?

Observation of this sacred garden became a basic task of the monastery, and it was a signal honor when a novice was deemed by the master of the novitiate to be observant and alert enough to be entrusted with membership in the Rota Hortensis, the staff of the garden. In fact most of the monks who were Watchers of the World (another name for the staff) were older, smart, knowing the names of many things.

Year after year the garden flourished and withered, dried out, boiled over with blossoms, was flooded with mud, hailed flat, april'd back to life again. Long before the oldest of the Rota passed away, a Regula or rulebook had been written, to secure uninterrupted perception of the garden, and the even more vital task of protecting it from forces of destruction or innovation—which in this context were almost the same. As the garden began, so it had to go on.

Fierce heretics arose who wanted to protect the garden by building walls around it, or erecting a dome of glass and amber and precious stones over so holy a place, or delving a fosse around it, or a moat dappled with swans. It took all the holy efforts of skilled interpreters and all the energy of communal prayer to win through to a certainty that the first way was best, leave it alone. Leave it alone to leave it alone.

Eventually controversy died down, and generations of monks were content to observe, annotate, observe, record, reflect the events or non-events of the sacred garden inside its simple shabby perimeter, whose cotton string was renewed every year on the twenty-first of July, feast of Saint Arbogast the Irishman, Bishop of Strassburg in Merovingian times, and called Hermit of the Sacred Forest.

Nothing more. Nine hundred square feet, a hundred twenty feet of string, four pinewood stakes, one monk. Every day.

Every year the Annals of the Garden were compiled, summarized every decade, published every century in full, with a digest of remarkable observations. Trees rose, trees fell, the mean temperature of the continent rose and fell, comets scribbled in the sky and went away, hurricanes came, droughts and floods and great winds, locusts, mice, moths. Several times the monastery itself was overrun by enemies of God or enemies of the State or starving peasants, and some of these times the garden too was bothered or violated—but that too, the monks reasoned, is just part of what happens. Let the garden take care of itself, they felt and sometimes spoke. A few of them may even have thought: Let the garden take care of us.

The garden is strong, the garden is enduring, and it endures because it changes.

Reflecting on this consoling but challenging fact, Brother Guido shielded his eyes from the rough October wind, and from inside his cowl noted the quiet agitation in the garden, the dried milkweed shivering its fluff under the wind's buffeting. He tried to keep track of the number of pods cracking open, but began to lose his way among the numbers. Counting always made him sleepy, an occupational hazard of those who tell their prayers on smooth-worn beads of horn or olive wood. He began to doze, struggling against it only a little, guessing reasonably that the precise number of milkweed pods chivvied into generosity is less important than: *wind blew, milkweed flew*, which is all he would write down later in any case. As he faltered ever further along sleep's road, he began to allow the consolations of his belief to seep through his mind, he began to think about this garden, this very sacred garden he had spent many years of his life observing with such care, he began to wonder if perhaps the garden is not the real garden after all, and maybe only that vast, frightening and interminable world outside the little white string was the real garden, and he, and his mother and father and abbot and all his brethren and their sisters and cattle and flies on the wall and soldiers at the gate and lepers beneath the hedge and harlots and scientists and ministers of state, yes and the bishops and cardinals and the Pope himself, servant of the servants of God, and God, God himself, himselves, all, all of them were just what happened, would never stop happening, ever, to the most sacred garden. Almost all the way there, Brother Guido could feel himself shrink back from something, something that might be right or might be wrong, but something that did him no good to think. He woke, or almost woke, in a curious stillness, looked into his garden and asked himself, Where is the wind?

III

Trigonometry

or, The Autopsychography of My Life

———————◦———————

T HE READER IS URGED to regard with welcoming alertness *any images, of whatever sort,* that may happen to arise in mind as the following chapter headings are read. Such images are the actual substance of the narrative proposed, and the text's only purpose is to solicit their arousal in the reader's mind. The images in your mind constitute the meat of what happened to me.

CHAPTER 1

Before I was young

CHAPTER 2

Becoming stricter in my inclinations I explore angles of incidence.

CHAPTER 40
Hydrangeas on the hillsides. Thrown by a horse.

CHAPTER 41
Around the world on the Contrapunctus,
while I still can!

CHAPTER 42
I resign from my several offices, and resolve to write
the story of my life. Learning to write.

CHAPTER 43
An Excursus on Nietzsche.

CHAPTER 44
I take leave of the patient Reader.

Two Towns

TELLAMASON

L ESS DREARY THAN IT LOOKS. The cooks have figured out ways of using stones for spices, and the town is full of aromas strange to us. At every corner there's a cauldron with soup bubbling, goat or degu or guinea fowl, some yucca and some okra, and then an assortment of big round stones heated in the fire below the cauldron. These are then carefully slipped into the stew, each one bringing its own flavor. Each corner has its own combination of stones, its own characteristic taste. It doesn't bear thinking about, the minerals that might be in these soups, but they taste good. Very good in fact, especially the degu stew, a small rat with a hairy tail. Certain unscrupulous vendors are rumored to use common rat instead, but since only a skilled anatomist can distinguish the animals, we are not worried. Worry is the one ingredient the traveler should leave behind. The soups are valued for the distinctive flavors of the stones, alone and in combination. Vendors, families of them, generations of them, preserve the secrets of their spices, perform their *wedding of the stones* in plain sight every day. Public secrets. No more hidden than, and just as impossible to imitate as, the famous smile of a famous actress we see every day on the cover of a magazine we stare at and do not read.

AGATE CITY

MOST PEOPLE arrive by bus but we chose to cycle over the long causeway from the other side of the Casubayou River, past the ruins of Smithtown and the old bog-iron works where the Confederate bayonets were made. We stayed in the Globo Hotel, unless we read the weathered sign wrong. We tried out our travellers' Portuguese but the people all spoke English, sort of. The most interesting thing in town, and why we'd bothered with the detour, was the Etheridge Museum. Here we saw taxidermy exhibits and dioramas dedicated to the various hybrid creatures bred by Emmanuel S. Etheridge, an early experimenter in animal husbandry, second president of the State Agricultural College (at Finsburg), as well as Lieutenant-Governor during the administration of Marvin B. Sweet (1897-1901). We were most moved by the skeleton of the Hound-Hog, which sepia photographs revealed as a formidable beast, big tusks, big chest, lank belly, seemingly standing as tall as a man's waist. "The fidelity of the Dog with the voracity of the Swine," was the stated, inexplicable, goal. The animal proved incapable of breeding. Not so the Rank, a cross that turned out to be so fertile that it had to be exterminated throughout the county. Stimulated by the hope of combining the voluptuous fur of the mink with the self-maintaining independence of the rat, Dr Etheridge in fact produced a huge, coarse-haired rat with the savage instincts typical of the mustelidae, a sort of hyperactive weasel. Even now specimens are said to survive in garbage dumps and derelict commercial zones. We thought we spotted one as we cycled back across the river next day, after a night of many dreams, including one in which the Bank of England had sunk deep below the sea, long pikes and sturgeons nosing through its vaults of gold.

The Tureen

⟐

IMAGINE A COUNTRY where every morning each able-bodied householder puts out two flags: one is the national ensign (blue, with an intricate golden device running along the hoist), the other a flag of one's own choosing. Each house will have several.

Imagine that the morning on which we choose to look out from our own windows, before we have given a moment's thought to what personally chosen banner we ourselves should run up, we squint a little to see across the way, and through the pleasant though not at this time blossoming fruit trees, we note that our neighbor has hoisted, beside the regrettably slightly faded national flag—blue dyes pale so quickly—a simple white flag on which, in vivid, dragon green, a soup tureen seems to welcome unseen diners. Streamers of steam rise from the bowl, thin curlicues of red. Embroidery, it looks like. They writhe in the low wind that moves the flag gently beyond the quince leaves.

Pretty as all this might be, it puzzles us. We have never seen the flag of the tureen before. Conjecture comes quickly. They are having a dinner party. Or the husband has left home for another woman, has repented of his folly and has called his wife eleven times in the past thirty-six hours and finally has induced her to take him back, and now in token of her relenting she has raised this hospitable banner. Yet a tureen, while signifying welcome and domesticity, scarcely offers the sort of embrace a penitential husband must require. Or it may in fact imply precisely this, that he is permitted to come home, but must expect that the wife's marital obligations will be confined, for the present at least, to seeing to his supper. Though why a tureen? A tureen implies amplitude, ancient dignity of domestic custom, serenity of mealtime, honored authority. One ladles, another receives. Yet more than all that, a tureen implies multiplicity; that great and costly piece of Spode we imagine when we hear the word 'tureen' is in fact no more than a Victorian embodiment of the ancient cauldron of plenty—plenty of soup, for plenty of people. So more must be being welcomed than one husband alone, however sinful, however contrite. We revert to our initial surmise: a dinner party is in the offing, and we have not been invited.

Now a flag is a vexing thing. Pretty it may be, or coarse, or elegant, ancient Dannebrog or newfangled gaudy bunting of tomorrow's next Balkan republic. Beyond the aesthetic appeal of the cloth itself, we realize that any flag is a provocation, perhaps even an insult. It proclaims its difference, its distance from us, its contentment with its own apartness. A flag is smug. How annoyed the sky must be, to have so many and various flags thrust up into it. But we retreat from such anthropomorphic, as we think we have heard it called, projection, and recognize that it is we who have been insulted. It is into our own visual space, if we may be permitted to claim it, that this soupy flag has lofted its mark.

It is a wrong we must redress. We hurry to the closet under the stairs where our flags are stowed. We select first the quite new national flag, blue as morning glories, carry it outside and clip it to the line, hoist it to the top of its pole. It rides the morning. We return to the hallway, thinking hard and clearly. Of the nine flags we have at our disposal, only two seem appropriate: a proud trotting black wolf on a silvery field, or a mailed fist grasping the hilt of a sword, the blade of which disappears into a cloud from which lightning bolts zigzag in all directions. The first will tell our neighbor: we do not care that we have not been invited to your boring party. Soup indeed. We are happier alone, free in our own world. The second will say: do not think a day of reckoning will never come. We stand idle a few moments, deciding between the display of indifference or the promise of revenge. We are inclining to the sword, but the wolf is lean and potent.

As we think about these matters, the telephone rings. It is our neighbor. Our neighbor has seen us hoist the national flag, and reasons from this that we are up and about. Our neighbor had awakened this morning, it is explained, from a vivid dream. The dream seemed like an instruction to our neighbor to arrange a gathering this very night, to which a number of people would be summoned. Would we ourselves consent to come, last-minute as the whole business must seem, and indeed is?

How is your husband, we ask. The neighbor seems surprised but not upset by the question. The husband is working in the garden at this very moment, setting ranunculus bulbs under a cold frame. This seems to us unnecessarily precise, and therefore rather suspicious, but we say nothing. We are in fact pausing to consider the invitation. Evidently sensing our hesitation, our neighbor adds some interesting conditions: please do come, and it should be clear that while there will be lots to eat and drink, this is not as such a dinner party. The food is in the background, our neighbor explained. The real point of the gathering is to create a neighborhood council to deal with spiritual issues. Our children are being exposed to influences of all sorts, from the most unreliable sources, as well as being bombarded with visual materials that deal with vampires and demons and diabolic possession and transmutation and reincarnation and other improper ways of thinking about what is after all our shared world. Our neighborhood, in fact. Tonight's gathering is to study and gather evidence, to create several committees, to decide what is to be done. It will be, the dream had insisted, the first of several neighborhood meetings, each devoted to one particular aspect of this unwelcome new information that comes flooding in all the time, doesn't it. Tonight's focus group would concern itself with alchemy. That is why the Green Athanor flag is flying in the driveway right now, did we notice.

We do not know much about alchemy, we admit, but we had seen the flag. We admit further that we did not quite know what to make of it. We are glad there is an explanation. We are glad someone is doing something about these problems. Though we are not sure we were really very aware of the problems to begin with.

The Plumber

H IS FATHER AND HIS grandfather had been too.
Maybe it was time for something new, but there is
no need for new things in houses. Getting water in, getting
ordure out, that is all that's ever needed. If all he has to do
is keep things flowing, what scope is there for the grand
designs he feels stirring inside him? Those too have to be
gotten out, given play. As years pass, he spends a lot of time
in discussing his feelings and projects as he works, talking
to the pipes, the old ones, copper and brass and even lead,
that he finds in the houses he comes to thaw or sweat, or to
the new ones of copper and plastic that he snakes through
rafters and under baseboards. He sings to the pipes, talks
to the pipes, rubs his hands on them, up the length or
round the bore, smoothly, rhythmically, coaxing the pipes,
talking to them, whispering into them even, humming,

singing, complaining of this and that, the pain of love, the losses, the boredom of Sunday afternoon, the smell of human waste mingling with the hot solder, the blow-torch, the flux. He sings into the pipes and the pipes remember. He lives till he dies, the way we do, but the people who live in the houses where he works will sometimes wake up in the night and say *Isn't that music, I hear music*, and the husband will answer, *Go to sleep, that's only the pipes.*

Woman with Dog

B UT HANDS WERE STILL holding her waist, tight as ever, so how could she be alone?

Tentatively she squirmed to see if she could free herself from the grasp, but the hands held firm. But she heard the voice again in her mind: Do you want me to let you go?

And she knew that was the last thing she wanted, no, no, don't let me go.

That is a good decision, it seemed to say. It's when you're looking that you can't find. You found the dog without looking for it.

The dog, she wondered?

The dog is your third star—a hot red star that burns its way towards you. All day you see it play around your feet, or, its candlepower quenched, snooze at the foot of your bed in the night. That is because you take it for granted in that quiet lovely way people have with animals, and that stars have with us. Lukette is really the star around which you move—you are the third planet out from that brightness, and the third planet is always the earth.

I am the earth, she thought, with a dull, quiet, comfortable feeling.

But then some skepticism roused in her. How can she be a dog and a star, be asleep at my feet and burning in the sky? If I'm the third planet out, where are the other two?

But it did not answer her. She kept still, and thought about it, tried counting things. Maybe the numbers mean something in themselves, maybe they're not just imaginary ideas used for counting real things. Maybe there's really something like twoness, threeness, oneness.

Then she started worrying, am I just a satellite of my dog? Just something that turns around that center? Is the sun my master? I hate this earth business, sometimes, this horny earth that needs heat and light and love, I hate this loud and bossy sun.

Then the voice was speaking again, cutting through all her feelings—

I am the fourth star, it said.

It spoke out loud, and the sound of the voice was shocking, but what it said was even more surprising.

But I thought the stars were in my bag, in my grasp?

Open your hands, it suggested.

She looked down and saw that all this while her hands had been clenched, and ached now with the tension of that pressure. Why was she holding tight? She felt her palms warm and red and full of discomfort, and suddenly splayed out her fingers fast.

Instantly the pressure round her waist and hips disappeared. It was as if she had been holding herself, then let herself go.

Are you there? Are you really anybody?

The voice spoke just as calmly as before, Yes, of course I'm here. It's not in your hands you hold yourself.

Where am I, then, if not in your hands?

I have no hands yet, not until you give them to me.

Oh this is all too much, she said, or thought she said. This is too much, too vague, too many numbers, too many things happening or not happening. All my life I thought there were things I needed, and places I needed to go to, and people I needed to have near me. But every time I claim anything here, you tell me I'm wrong.

I never said you were wrong, the voice said. You are far from wrong, and you understand perfectly well that constellations of the mind are what we're talking about. We're not talking about things and places and people. I'm not a people. I'm not an interesting place you can go to, like Africa or Brazil.

I'm tired of all this, I just want to lie down in my bed, she thought. And then she thought, this is like making love forever and never coming, it seems all beautiful and lyrical and forever and then after a while it just seems tired and irritating. I want to come! she thought.

It felt stern inside her, it felt as if a judgment had been passed, it felt as if her heart were frowning. But the voice was just as mild and kindly as before.

If you came, then you'd have to be somewhere. And then you'd have to go. This is not a rhythm that has an end. Where you are now, you think of it as floating, and floating means: not here and not there, not going and not coming. It's just as image or an idea, to show you how you are.

Aren't I in the sky, though?

We're all in the sky.

At those words she felt a sudden swoon of vertigo, so sudden that she closed her eyes against it the way we do when we have to deny the world outside just to be faithful to the mind we are. Vertigo, and then it just as suddenly stopped.

She felt a hard pressure under her elbows, and she opened her eyes. It took her a moment to grasp that she was in a window, leaning on the sill, her own bedroom, leaning on her elbows on the window sill, and her neck was stiff from looking up into the blank sky while her body was bending down. She lowered her head and there was the lawn in front of her, with her dog looking up at her. Am I the moon she's going to bark at, she thought.

She looked down further, and saw her nightgown, the little pale beige stain at the waistline where the wine spilled last night. Golden wine from Hungary, so sweet, tasting like valleys and shadow. Golden shadows.

She was conscious of disappointment, a quiet kind of shock, to be back here in her bedroom. Where are the stars I cared so much about?

Around she turned and looked back into the gloom of the bedroom. Her husband was asleep, curled into a gentle question mark beneath the white woolen blankets. Across the middle of his body lay outspread, rising and falling a little with his breathing, a faded red brocade they had bought in North Africa.

I follow this everywhere, she thought, even here, even to this strange destination, my own house.

And would she still be able to hear that voice inside her, if it was inside? Did she want to hear it?

Whether or not she did, the voice was speaking in her already.

Do you think your husband is a star, Star Number Five? That's up to you to decide.

She walked over the smooth cold polished floor and sought the relief of the furry rug by the bedside. She looked down at her sleeping husband's face. Why does everybody look the same when they're asleep?

That had always haunted her, as if sleep were one same country we all live like equals in, and everybody is the same there, same face, same expression.

She studied his face, trying to see how he was different, different from every other sleeper. He's only different when he's awake, she thought. Tenderness for him flowed in her, but the voice was speaking.

That is the single mystery of sleep, to teach us to wake up.

She spoke out loud, trying the answer the voice: we're only different when we're awake, only after we've awakened are we who we really are.

Off her shoulder she let the nightgown slip and slide to the floor. Then she stood in the cold morning light, shivering a little.

Saving the Moon

THE TOWN WAS SMALL but I still was able to find a bed and breakfast with a clean room on the third floor. In summer it would have been dim with leafage by grace of the maple so close to my window. Now I had an interesting gridwork of branches to frame and section a big view of the town's one street, stretching far into the houseless snowbound prairies beyond, into the same sky that was also, so strikingly close, right over me, around me, in this low town. The wallpapers were chintz, cabbage roses, mauve. I dislike looking at chintz, but I always sleep well in a room with flowers on the wall.

I expected to spend most of my time taking care of the business that brought me to the town, no need to bother you with that, a will and a codicil, an argument, a family divided, nothing close to my heart but it had to be done.

So I didn't worry about the cabbage roses getting on my nerves.

Luck brought me to the town at the time of the full moon, and each night the snow glistened tender dry crystalline, still not much soiled by traffic, of which there was little enough at the best of times, they tell me. Now the plowed snow was piled so deep beside the sidewalks that pedestrians felt embraced and guided by these quiet white wings. Or I did, since I'm from a place where we don't see much snow.

I ate my dinner late, at the Blue Moon Café, every town used to have one, I'm not sure that most do any more, but this one had, and the food was fair. I don't worry much about food; sometimes I think I eat mostly to be sociable. I'd eat at the counter, usually, and talk to the waitress and anybody else around. That way I'd get a feel for the town. That can help in my line of work.

So it happened that I learned of the business that was upsetting the town these days. The barber, who spent most of his hours in the café, and the old hunter, who never went out hunting while I was in the town, and the waitress did most of the talking. I listened and learned.

It seemed that a darkish fellow, swarthy as a gypsy said the old hunter, had come to town recently, driving a big fancy RV, where he slept and spent most of his days. The traveling home had a satellite dish on the roof, and even a little windowbox with plastic geraniums in it. Every morning he would come to this café, and begin to talk.

Now I always took my breakfast at the B&B where I stayed, meager as the fare was there—I had paid for it, and I would eat it. So I never got to hear the Gypsy, as they called him. So I have to take their word for what he said.

At first he talked generally about this and that, history. He seemed to have a lot to say about Napoleon and Hitler, and about the banks, and how the government controlled, or was it was unable to control, what he called the velocity of money in the world. After a while, when people had gotten used to his know-it-all ways, he started to tell them about the moon. It was a few days before the full of the moon that he began to tell them that this next full moon was the last full moon they would ever see. It seems an ancient cycle of the Guarany Indians down in Paraguay (from whom the Jesuits had stolen all their wisdom centuries ago) proclaimed that this very month would be the End of Time.

Nobody took this very seriously, since Time is always ending, and the Last Judgment is always around the corner, and so on. But the particular way the so-called Gypsy talked about this began to get under the skin of his listeners. He didn't have the usual triumphant certainty that most doomsayers exult in; he didn't seem convinced or trying to convince. He just seemed sad.

Eventually somebody, the waitress from what I could gather, asked him Well, isn't there anything we can do? The man just shook his head, closed his eyes, sighed, and shook his head again.

But the next morning when he came in, his eyes were brighter, and as soon as he had mopped up the last of the imitation maple syrup with the last of his pancakes, he told them that he had been thinking. He had sat up late thinking and thinking, and finally he got the idea that what one Indian could do, another Indian could undo, and he brought to mind an old Lakota medicine man he used to know.

As soon as he had this thought, he got out of his snug little camper and climbed into the driver's seat and started driving. It was almost midnight, but he kept going—drove till three a.m. and got to the little settlement in the middle of nowhere where his old Indian lived. Woke him up in the middle of the night, explained the problem, got the answer, and drove back, got back to our town at first light and here he was with the good news.

This was the story: The old Indian had said that there was only one chance. We had to make a big offering to the Goddess of the Dawn. See, for us Indians, the Moon is a Man, a lonely old man in the middle of the sky. Many years ago, before the white man, even before the red man came to America, the moon used to be bright every night. We had the beautiful sun maiden in the daytime and the handsome moon boy at night, and each was bright as their nature was, bright all the time. But with the passing years, the moon boy got older and older, became the moon man, then an old man. He's so old now. Old. That is why he's barely able, nowadays, to be fully bright even one night a month. He's dying, dying, and now the time has come. Yes, this is the last full moon there will ever be. After this, the moon will just fade away.

Now we could all put up with that, we've got electricity and such for our night time, and television, and candles and all sorts of things. But the big trouble is this: once the moon is gone, the sun will go too. Little by little the sun will lose her power, and the world will get cold and dark all the time, it will be like this in July, snow on the fields and dark at three o'clock in the afternoon. The Indians have always known this was coming.

And you know how Indians are (the Gypsy is said to

have reported), they are fatalistic. They know that the dying of the world is part of the world's way, and no business of theirs to interfere. Nevertheless, the old Indian had said, they could stop the dying of the moon if they wanted to. How could they do that? Well, because the sickness of the moon over all these thousand thousand years has been a kind of love sickness – the moon has not been in love with his proper mate the sun, but instead has become infatuated with the shy, fleeting goddess of the dawn. And dawn won't have him, won't even let him lie down an hour in her deerskin sleeping bag with her. If dawn would let the moon love her, why, then the moon would grow strong again. But the moon is on his last legs now, and this infatuation of his, and this refusal of hers, is going to plunge our world into the dark. But that's how it goes.

What could we do, the Gypsy had demanded. Maybe we could ask the dawn to take moon into her bed, just once maybe, just to slake the hunger of his long appetite, that might work. But how could we persuade the dawn to do anything? We can't even make her sunny when we're tired of winter. Well, said the old Lakota, my grandfather used to say that the sun liked gold, and the moon liked pearls and shells, but the dawn liked silver. Maybe if we offered a lot of silver to the dawn, maybe then she'd relent, and we'd all be saved.

Then how much silver became the issue. And how to offer it? Where does dawn come to find our offerings? The old man said that if some white men, who own all our sacred land away from us, could offer say ten pounds of silver, drive it out onto the prairie far away and leave it for the dawn to find it, far away from anybody, he thought that would work.

That was the story the stranger had puzzled the waitress with, and the hunter, and the barber. Every afternoon when I came in for a snack, then every night when I came in for supper, I'd find them talking about it. Other townspeople got involved in the discussions. There was a lot of skepticism, which I, as an outsider, naturally shared. The general line ran: every month the moon wanes, disappears, comes again. It's called waxing and waning, it's always been that way and always will. The world doesn't change its rules, said the policeman. Things go on the way they always do, said the schoolteacher. But the lay teacher at the Sunday school wasn't too sure. He began to remember passages in the Holy Scriptures that could be read as having a special and sinister reference to our current anxieties. For example, he reminded his listeners, there is that passage in Revelations where the Moon is rolled up like an old scroll and taken away. The skeptics couldn't say much to this, either out of sudden doubt, or decent respect for the holy book.

Every evening I'd check in, and listen to the latest stages of speculation. And every evening the moon would be a little less visible, a little less bright than the night before.

The Gypsy was gone for a few days, and when he came back one morning, I never did see him, a strange thing, but he'd always be gone by the time I'd get a little hungry in the afternoon, when he did come back he seemed more worried than ever before. He'd been back to see his old Indian friend, and learned that there was not much time left to do something.

You see, he explained, it's not as if the moon will go on going through its phases as before, gradually getting a little less bright month by month. No, it's worse than that.

This is the end of the cycle, the whole thing. After the dark of the moon this month, this very month, the moon will never come back.

The moon will never come back. Even I was shocked when I heard it.

We've got to do something, some people said. Others said the whole thing was nonsense, of course the moon would get dim and then get bright again, and in a few weeks would be the glorious full moon of the new year, and so on. But the worriers kept worrying out loud.

What if you're wrong, and this old Indian is right. They've been here for thousands of years, they can tell when things are going the same or going different. Then the old doctor, a man whose hands trembled a bit but who was still in practice, the town's only doctor, he who had been on the skeptical side all week long, now shook his head and said I wonder, I wonder. It occurs to me that the moon is not as bright as it was when I was a boy. Maybe your eyes are getting old, somebody said. Yes, they are, he said, but that doesn't matter, because the sun is brighter than it used to be. That silenced them for a while. Then the waitress, who read the paper when business was slack, wondered if it wasn't global pollution that made the moon seem dimmer to the doctor. No way of telling, said the barber. Then the hunter said, Well, we've got to do something.

Nobody said anything more that day. But the next afternoon when I came in, everybody was talking about the price of silver, and how to buy it. Someone looked it up online and discovered its cost per ounce. The barber, who was up on technology, wondered when the old Indian said Ten Pounds of Silver, did he mean troy weight that jewelers use, or avoirdupois weight, that everybody else uses—a troy pound has only twelve ounces in it, but an avoirdupois, as you all know, has sixteen. Ten troy pounds of silver will cost us a lot less than ten avoirdupois pounds. That's true, said the policeman, but what does an Indian know about troy weight? Good point, said the barber.

So this was the first time when there had appeared in the Blue Moon Café's conversation the idea that they themselves were going to have to buy the silver. Sixteen ounces of silver made one pound, one hundred and sixty ounces made ten pounds of silver. The waitress was trying to use the cash register calculator to reckon these sums. Over a thousand dollars, she said. About fourteen hundred dollars, said the doctor, who was still good with figures.

The next few days were spent gathering the money, collecting sums from everybody they could persuade. The policeman used his cruiser to visit every farm in thirty miles, making sure everybody had a chance to do his civic duty. Save the Moon! was inscribed on a big banner in the café window, and then, two days later, on an even bigger banner stretched across the main street from a lamp post over to the corner of the drug store building.

Every night the moon was dwindling, gibbous, then fading to crescent. Fortunately, by the night of the last quarter, all the money had been raised; I had put in my share too, though I didn't believe in all this at all, not me, but I liked these people a little, and couldn't refuse them when they asked.

Now the problem was how to turn the money into silver. Not easy to buy precious metal. The nearest bank, eighteen miles away, could not help, never had to buy any, didn't know how it was done. Everybody seemed stumped. I knew you could buy silver or even gold at

certain international banks in New York or Chicago, and
maybe jewelers in smaller cities handled it as well. But I
had no time to spare from my work, so I waited to see
what would happen. I had done my share already.

Reluctantly, the Gypsy next morning had volunteered
to help now that time was running out. He admitted that
it was he who had first told us about the danger, and so he
should be brave enough to carry through the mission, if we
wanted to entrust it to him. There had not been much discussion of this, especially since he was sitting right there.
So in the end, the policeman, who was treasurer, had
turned over the money to him, in cash. Then the Gypsy,
who was no Gypsy, by the way, of course not, it was just his
dusky skin that made people call him that, no, his name
was Slavic, really, though they said he didn't look Polish or
anything, so the Gypsy had taken out a big survey map of
this part of the state, and asked the people to help him decide where the best place to leave the silver would be. They
argued about this for a while, finally settling on a piece of
grassland in the northwest corner of the map, not all that
far from where we were. After all, we wanted to get the first
benefit of the offering. The schoolteacher had composed a
little letter with a poem in it that his class had collaborated
to write, a little poem asking the moon to fulfill his heart's
delight come make bright again our night. This letter was
given to the Gypsy (though a copy was mounted on the
café wall, beside the cash register). Then he had set out on
his mission, leaving them the map, with a big cross marking exactly where the silver was to be placed.

He left that night. After a few days, he had not come
back. He should have reported back, the policeman said.
Maybe he's still finding the silver, the waitress thought

out loud. I wonder if he's going to get it and get there on time. Maybe we should get in touch with that old Indian, what was his name? He never said, and never said where he lived.

People began to doubt and worry out loud now. Maybe he had taken the money and just gone away, or maybe (thought the hunter) maybe he did get the silver, but went home to his own place or his own people to plant it there, so they would get the blessing of the moon.

What blessing is that, the lay preacher wanted to know. Whatever blessing we're getting, said the waitress, the moon will come back.

I had a late supper there the night after the dark of the moon. I'd been in the town two weeks, and my business was almost finished. I had supper with the lawyer, in fact, who never usually ate in the café. They all knew him, and he them, but they didn't specially socialize, so there was less talk than usual. People were worried and depressed. What if he hadn't found the silver? What if he hadn't found the right place? And a worse thing too: what if the old Indian was crazy, and the dawn wouldn't give in to the moon? What if there were no way of changing the destiny of the sky?

The lawyer and I talked about various things of no consequence, the way people do. All round us I could feel, and share, the distress of the townspeople. Then suddenly a boy I didn't know at all came bursting in, shouting Come out, come out and see! And we all left our plates of stew and hurried out into the street and looked up where the boy was pointing. There, low in the west, was the slimmest sickle of new light. The moon had come back! Our silver had done the trick! All at once, with one voice, we gave a great cry of rejoicing.

IV

La Tache Vertigineuse

THERE WAS A SOMEONE reading at the table in the underground library; though pale, and wearing clothes subdued in hue, he was made to seem colorful, even gaudy, by contrast with the ashen table at which he sat under the bleak indifferent but powerful scrutiny of the fluorescent lights caged above. A deep book lay in front of him, its straw-colored pages sprawled; the book did not have to be held, but lay on the desk obediently open. He seemed to read it attentively, an elbow to either side of the book, his hands nestled round his face as he read. Undirected as the light was, it still cast a shadow across him, one that darted down the long slope of his neck from hairline to a vanishing point in his pale sweater. I stared at this shadow and tried to discern the character and destiny of the reading man by means of it. But the longer I stared, the more I felt I was beginning to sway and grow dizzy, to be falling, slowly but ineluctably, forward towards him, towards the shadow he sported on his skin. Into the shadow I was spinning, my head careening around the swimming room, I seemed to fall forward into that shadow and consented to, wanted, and I fell. Everything we ever see is an abyss.

The Skirt

━━━━━━━⟫•⟪━━━━━━━

T HE INTERVIEWER WAS beginning to grow uneasy
about the way the writer kept looking at her lap. Not
staring at it, but looking away and looking back, and the
eyes dwelling, then looking away. Then looking back as if
to make sure it was still there. She was still there.

They had been at it for over an hour, and the writer had
been very forthcoming, helpful even. He had carefully
guided her often unformed questions, questions she had
thrown together hurriedly in a local library when she got
this assignment. Actually she hadn't found much about
the man, and honestly she hadn't read any of his many
books. But she didn't tell him that, and he didn't ask. She
wasn't sure whether he simply assumed she naturally had
read them, or whether he was wise enough to realize that
not many people read books of any kind. In any case, he

made no allusions to his own writings except in the most explicit or general ways, and seemed to expect no recognition from her.

So often the interviewer herself seems on the line. But he had somehow set her mind at rest, and made her feel at ease. He answered fully, courteously, and often led to new areas she might, if she chose, ask about. And often she did.

Their rapport then was considerable, and she felt gratitude and admiration for the way he had made her feel comfortable. Only this staring at her lap business, that bothered her.

The interviewer had gotten lots of material, and thought, in a kind of wicked impulse, that maybe she should make some allusion to this behavior that was making her uneasy. She had her interview, what was there to lose? And it might bring up some interesting outburst from him—he'd been so controlled!

"There's one thing, if you forgive me, there's one thing that's kind of troubling for me. I notice you keep looking at me, I mean at my knees, my lap. I just thought I'd mention it."

The man looked at her, and she could see a little color flush the pale skin below his eyes. Was he angry, or blushing, embarrassed? What a pale man, pale skin, great shock of tousled silver hair. But the eyes seemed just as friendly, amused even, as before.

"Forgive me," he said, delicately stressing the pronoun. "Not your lap, no… No, but you have a nice lap. Only people have laps, have you ever thought of that? No other animal has a lap. We are human, among other reasons, because we can sit down and acquire a useful and civilized lap. An ape can sit down, but then he just has two legs, two knees stuck out in front of him. Not a lap, a lap is a single thing, a singular thing, a union of left and right, a unity. A soft and pleasing unity, too. No, sorry, I'm sorry, I wasn't looking at it, your lap I mean, I was looking at your skirt."

He stopped talking, and she thought he wasn't going to say anything else. Did he think that explained anything? She looked down at her skirt and checked it quickly —unstained, not too wrinkled, snug but not all stretched looking, and had not crept too far up from the knee, and wasn't gapping under the thigh. What was wrong with the skirt?

"Your skirt reminded me of something. Sorry. Of a, another skirt, another woman, another year. Sorry."

Again he fell silent. Such silence was unexpected, since through the whole interview he had been quite voluble, and in fact she had had quite a job in keeping up with him, keeping track of what he said. Fortunately she had her little tape recorder running—but would she be able to make head or tail of what he was talking about, later?

"Lincoln Center, and they're all dead."

He had spoken abruptly, and in a low voice. She had no idea what he meant. Had he said something before that she hadn't caught?

"Excuse me? What?"

"I'm sorry," he said, "you couldn't know. The skirt. Let me tell you. It was important to me, once. Once is a long time, sometimes." His voice trailed off, and then: "A long once…"

She smiled at him in what she hoped was an encouraging way. The gappedness of his talk now, his uncertainty, was promising, she thought, as if she were really getting to something. Something deep. But did she want anything like that? She just needed a thousand words or so for the lead article in the "People" section that weekend. She didn't need the story of his life.

"It was forty years ago, you understand. I was in a bus, going uptown, along Eighth Avenue. Eighth Avenue was then, as it is now, a poor place, full of shabby people, shabby stores, and besides all the terminals and fast food joints, it was also the main street for neighborhood, all the poor whites and latinos who lived in the crowded streets running west to the river. I was very poor in those days. I remember a place by the old Penn Station where you could eat a full meal, blue plate special with roll and butter for 35 cents. Fried eggplant it was, and two veg. I always got macaroni as one of the vegetables. Do you know New York?"

Of course she knew New York. Everybody knows New York. It's only a few hundred miles away. She nodded, annoyed, but wanting not to show it.

"It was summertime, a typical New York summer, hot and sticky and smelly and sexy, the old leather seats on the buses stuck to your skin, the open windows let in the hot air, the exhaust, the smell of cuchifritos on every corner. We were in the 20s or the 30s, I don't remember. Maybe we'd just pulled away from 23rd street, and I was of course looking out the window. That's the great thing about buses."

She feared a long digression about busses, looking, cities, windows, but he kept going.

"And there she was. Right there, on the sidewalk, in front of a store, a girl, on the pavement, minding her young brothers and sisters, and flirting with other kids. A lot of kids there, but she was the center. She was the queen. She was tall, graceful, with wavy brown hair and a cute face, sort of Irish, green eyed, and a look that was overwhelmingly naughty, naughty, such an old word, not wicked, not mean, but daring and saucy and all those things, a girl standing out from the crowd. And she was wearing your skirt, a snug, smooth cocoa-colored gabardine, and you could tell she was proud of herself, and wanted to show herself, she knew it was danger, she knew it was worth the risk. She was a queen, I tell you, but I'm not sure of what. I saw her only for those few seconds as the bus went by, just a few seconds, but I knew her down to the bottom of my soul, not hers, there was more there than I could ever know. I knew she was wild, and wanton, and free. I could see she was poor, and in the trap of the city, a slum child, but with a wild spirit, and she would make her way—she was a girl who would do anything! And she could do it! God, those hips! They haunted me for hours, days. They still haunt me—there, in the poise of her, the slutty boldness of her clothes, in the meat of her, there was some terrible and glorious balance achieved, as if her hips were some great pendulum that ruled the earth. O I know I'm raving. But I've thought about that girl for forty years, and all the women I have loved and lived with, for all their loveliness, do not efface, and should not efface, that single glimpse of a wildness. Because she was *free*. She was the freedom of the body, a terrifying sensual freedom because I could see, anybody could see, there was nothing she wanted to be *but* free.

And do you know, I've never spoken of her, never till now. All my life. Your skirt, your skirt, and, to be honest,

I suppose, your hips, made me remember. Sorry, you don't need to hear all this stuff."

She was sad to hear him trail off that way, after the almost visionary excitement of the description. And she felt flattered that, after all these years, he had chosen her to be the one to whom he told so important a part of his mind's life.

And suddenly it all felt different. A wave of feeling, sheer feeling, washed over her, and she shared with him, for a moment, the power of that image, so swift, so lasting, that had so enthralled and, yes, energized him. In a dim way, she had the feeling that maybe all his books and so on had somehow come from that moment. From that woman. She felt a generosity towards him, one that surprised her a little, because she didn't really like this man very much. Maybe she ought to feel a little respect for all the work he'd apparently done. She had read the list of his books. Now she even forgot to smile when she spoke.

"It must be wonderful to have a memory in your mind like that. Something so intense at the bottom. Almost like something holy."

He just looked at her, as if what she said surprised him too. "Yes, I suppose it it. I was thinking about her the other day, this woman of my memory. I realized that she'd be close to sixty years old now, if she's alive. Probably drinks too much, has had too many kids, I don't know. She might even still live near Eighth Avenue, because she was the kind who didn't need to go anywhere or do anything to get free, she was free, and could do what she liked right there. Sixty years old, haggard, coarse. Or frail.

"I was living in the 60s then, where Lincoln Center is today. They tore down all the old brownstones, we used to live in a basement, we had a piano, they called it a garden apartment. My wife and I. She's dead now, that wife, long ago. That's what I was thinking the other day, they're all gone, the houses, the people. If I had gotten to midtown and gotten off the bus and gotten home, who could I have told about the girl in the skirt? My wife? Make her jealous, though she wasn't a jealous woman. I never spoke. And if I had, everyone I could have spoken to, they're all dead now, curious. Curious. I mean I'm not that old, but still they're all gone. I've outlived all the people I knew then, who I could have talked to. And I have to make an effort to remember them. But she's different. She's waiting there, part of the hot weather, part of the color scheme, part of the street. She still excites me."

It displeased her to hear this. She did not want to think of older people feeling sexual desire. Especially, while she was right here with him, she didn't want this man feeling desire. Not while she was wearing this fatal skirt. She wanted to change the subject, rather urgently.

"Are there other memories you have, like that? That's so interesting, to see something just once, and always remember it, and kind of use the memory. Other things like that?"

"Don't be afraid," he said. He seemed to read her anxiety. Why not, he was supposed to be so smart, a genius of some sort, a writer. Can writers be geniuses? Don't they just make things up?

But he was going on: "It's not just the girl, the skirt, the excitement of her wildness, or that she seemed to be so naked, naked in her clothes. It's that it's all gone. Everything is gone. I've held the memory for forty, forty-five years. Penn Station's gone, the West 60s are gone, the girl is gone, and everybody I knew then and there are gone. What good is the memory? What good is this intense pinpoint of awareness and excitement and desire, floating like, I don't know, like a speck of dust in sunlight, or like some floater in a sick eye, when everyone is dead. The memory kept nothing alive except itself."

The interviewer felt bold, and added:

"And maybe it kept you alive, too."

"Maybe it did. Yes, maybe it did. That's a nice idea, thank you for it. To owe one's life to a chance—not even an encounter. A glimpse. To live from a glimpse. Maybe that's what they felt, the ones who saw Christ passing through the roads on his business. Just a glimpse, and that's enough. Maybe. Thank you. I wonder if I'm worth it. Suppose you were that girl, what would you think?"

Alarmed, the interviewer froze. This was just the sort of connection she didn't want. But before she could answer, he went on:

"But of course, you've told me already what you would think. You told me the glimpse of her kept me alive. Yes, I think that's the truth. Of all the foods that keep us going, perceptions are the most important. Did you know that a man can live for fifty days without solid food, and five days without water, but not even for twenty-four hours without sense perceptions? A fact."

She felt reassured so hear him launch into this pedantic digression, and began thinking of winding up the interview. She kept hoping the tape would run out—its final click would be a good signal, and make it easy.

"You asked me about whether I had any other memories."

She was sorry she had, but she smiled, vaguely.

"Memory judges us. We stand accused by what we remember. This girl in her tight skirt—how shall I put that in the balance against Dante's vision of the young Beatrice, in garments white and red, on the bridge over the Arno? Doesn't the difference between the greatness of Dante's accomplishment and the scatteredness of all my own messy work show up already in each poet's dominant image? His Beatrice was white and red, was pure and youthful and apart, stood on a bridge, was herself the bridge between human love and godly love. And look at the image that chose me... And yet, we are both of the city, Dante and I, both poets, one great, one just able to keep one word coming out after another. Poets. Of the city."

He closed his eyes, and seemed to whisper to himself. "And yet I am, even I, I am a poet."

She thought of him mostly as a novelist and writer of short stories, and thought he might be quoting something. People who remember so much usually like to quote.

"Or Augustine," he said in a loud voice, "Saint Augustine. Did you ever read Saint Augustine? You're a reporter, I think you'd be interested in his *Confessions*. He was the very first person ever to write confessions, an autobiography told from the perspective of personal sin and imperfection slowly brought towards purification. The first interviewee, interviewed by himself. And he interviewed God, too. Because the whole *Confessions* is a story told to God. God is the you of the story."

Again the writer's voice trailed off.

Then he said, his voice strong again, "You are God!"

She waited. When people say things like that, it's better to wait and see what they mean. But he closed his eyes.

Some tenderness for him she felt. He seemed tired, full

of ideas but so tired. Maybe she should try to help him, he'd been helpful, she could ask, one can always ask.

"What are you thinking?"

He spoke without opening his eyes.

"Augustine was telling God about his sins, he was telling God about some pears he stole once. Do you remember the story? The pears grew on a tree over the wall, he climbed, he snatched, he ate. It was the color of the pears, the ripeness, the sweetness—everything we want. And stealing is reaching out and taking it. Stealing is taking God's world and making it just your own. But Augustine was talking about sin, his sin, all sin—all sin, of which this little kid stealing sweet pears from a neighbor is the type, the model. The paradigm. O my god, how we live the paradigm."

The reporter had no idea where this was headed. What did he mean, we live the paradigm?

"And I stole once too."

"Did you steal pears?" She asked just to show that she had been following his digression. If it was a digression.

'No, my dear, not pears. I stole an apple. I was a little boy, and was showing off, the way little boys do. My little friends and I wandered around a corner and there on the side street was a peddler's wagon, a wagon full of dusty red apples. The peddler was talking to some woman, his horse was sleeping in the sunlight, the peddler was leaning on the horse, the woman was asking him questions about the apples. I said to my companions: I am going to rob an apple. I didn't do it furtively, and I had spoken in a loud voice. Already I had some sense of the difference between stealing and robbing."

"What do you mean?" She was sorry she asked, for fear

he'd wander away from the story, not that it was much of a story.

"Stealing is furtive, robbing is bold. Thieves slip through the shadows, robbers stand on the highway."

She didn't think a little boy snagging a single apple from the back of a horse-cart was very bold, but she didn't say so.

"What happened then? Did he catch you?"

"Nothing happened. I think he saw me, the peddler, but he was too busy chatting up the woman. He may have waved us away, vaguely. Or I don't remember. Nothing really happened. But I am ashamed, ashamed."

"It doesn't seem so awful, it was just an apple, you were just a child."

He opened his eyes and looked at her at last.

"Ashamed. Then and now. Augustine, what did he do? He saw a golden fruit bursting with sensuality, sin and flesh and juice and yearning, a golden ripeness lost in the darkness of some neighbor's yard, and he climbed like an angel of desire, climbed up and seized it and ate and ate, and later felt the flame of guilt lick his secret places, the way it does, the way it does. That was Augustine. And what was I? The apple was dusty, hard, I never liked apples, I didn't even eat it, I threw it away, and felt ashamed. Ashamed at my folly—I was not in love with the fruit, the sweet, the sense; I was in love with the sin, in love with showing off. What god would even bother striking me down in my sin? Augustine wanted the fullness of lust and life, and seized it, sinned and repented. I wanted to show off. Paltry, that's what I was, I was paltry. Look at the magnitude of Augustine, and the paltriness of me. They appall me still. I am shamed by what I remember."

What could she say? He needed some soothing, but she didn't know how to do it. She didn't know what really bothered him—not getting the girl, not wanting the fruit? She tried to relieve his distress.

"I don't know, but it sounds to me as if you feel about that girl on the street the way Augustine felt about the pear."

"That is kind of you to say, and perceptive. Yes, that's true, that is how I felt, and how I still feel. He climbed his wall, and I'm still looking up into the twilight. It was twilight when I saw her, a hot, fading summer twilight."

"So you're not so different from Augustine."

"O my dear child, how sweet of you to say so. But it's not right, not at all. Except in one way: We are all equal before Memory. Hour after hour Memory keeps preaching the terrible insidious seductive doctrines of the past. They make us remember, and worse than that, make us think that what we remember was real, really real. All those beautiful recollections, *ricordanze*, yes, you look Italian, you know, memory makes us think all those beautiful memories are real, makes us think they are ours, makes us think that by knowing them we know ourselves. As if all I am is what I remember.

"And since everybody has memories, everybody is equal. How democratic it is! A rich man's childhood and a poor man's childhood are equivalent when the men are old and look back—every memory is just as far away, just as poignant, just as lost. Every memory is like every other memory, just as real, just as illusory. The bleak Dickensian childhoods of the poor (I know, I had one—at least I think I remember having had one!), the bleak childhoods of the poor are, when remembered in old age, just as riveting, just as full of precise and sensuous and overwhelmingly feelingful detail as the memories of the rich child who had everything. Maybe memory is all we ever have, and Memory, like death, makes us all equals."

That seemed interesting. She could use that. She could see it on a subhead in column, the Democracy of Memory. Is that too abstract for the paper? And she never really thought she looked Italian. But I have grey eyes, she wanted to tell him, couldn't he see?

She was shocked when he spoke, it was as if he had heard her thinking.

"Ah, don't you see, it is hopeless. Hopeless. All I do is see."

He looked over at the interviewer now, and smiled, simply, even shyly, she thought.

"We know so little about what goes on inside. Look at the two of us now—I am gazing into my mind and all I see is a girl on Eighth Avenue so long ago, my mouth dries and my breath comes quick as I see her in my mind's eye.

"And you, all you get to see is an old man remembering."

The Cryptanalyst

A<small>FTER A CERTAIN POINT</small> one day, drinking coffee in a coffee house and listening to a radio on the shelf behind the espresso machine playing a four-handed late piano andante of Mozart, he realized that Mozart was the only answer. Not that Mozart necessarily knew the answer—with such a genius, how could one be sure, but probably not. But Mozart himself was the answer. It came to him in one simple moment: take all the compositions Mozart ever wrote, and arrange them in strict order of their composition.

If the exact date was unknown, leave it aside for the moment.

Take the resultant opus, and play it, in order, listening first generally, then later carefully. Months it would take to do it consciously. Listen and note what the music said.

Study every parameter. Graph every pitch, every accidental, every dynamic marking, every variety of note, every expressive mark. Read in order the verbal text that accompanied cantata, motet, song, opera.

Graph after graph, statement after statement.

Take what you have heard and what you have before you as the encryption of a single text.

Decipher it.

From the gaps in the resultant clear text you will know where to fit in the many compositions without firm date, once these compositions have themselves been decoded according to the same cipher discovered in the whole corpus of sound.

He determined to devote his life to this decipherment. A hidden life it would have to be, dedicated to this great mystery, well-hidden in plain sight for two hundred years. No better code than the code that no one thinks is a code, he reflected. And he reflected on the life that would be his, all the work, copying, listening, playing, transcribing unrecorded pieces in some form he could play on his mother's old piano left to him after his parents died together in a plane crash on a hillside in Sardinia he had never seen. A small piano. A whole life he would spend. The thought of it exalted him and wearied him. He stared into his empty cup and wondered what would become of him. O my dear God, he thought.

The Secret

———❧·◦·❧———

THERE WAS A WIND and there usually wasn't. It was one of those days when the world seemed to be trying to tell him something. It had been trying so long, years and years, and today it was close. He was close to paying attention. The secret is released by paying attention. Releasing attention. He was trying to listen.

The secret somehow had to do with a sick old carpenter who kept missing work. A carpenter with a funny little scornful but abashed smile under a ratty grey mustache. The carpenter was going to the hospital.

He saw the carpenter's face in his mind's eye. The face was the same, old, mustache, little smile. Now the secret was close. Then he saw the carpenter as a young man, brown silly mustache of a young man. Silly preoccupations of a young man, so earnest, so wrong, so young.

A boy, even, going out with girls, choosing one or being chosen, getting married, living with her, an Irish girl, an Irish woman, getting old, a sick old Irish woman he lived with now, his wife in a wheelchair, the secret was very close now, the carpenter on his way to the hospital, his own body sick, he didn't know how, sick legs, kidneys, eyes, insides. The smile.

Everything was the same. That was close to the secret. A man was young and now he's old. No, that's the wrong way round. A man is old and once was young. That's closer, not right, nothing's right, the man is sick, he'll die, we all do, later or sooner, that's not the secret, that's common knowledge. But the secret is nearby. A man's life. Someone's life, someone's life is held together. What holds it together. What is the secret, that is the secret. He thinks he knows it now, archaic Greek *kouros* young boy statue smile. Old carpenter. Young man becoming carpenter. Making things. Looking at them in his mind's eye before he makes them. Not bothering to come to work. A dumb smile. Dying, Irish girls, sickness, telephones, excuses, hospitals, money. All quiet now. The wood is quiet. The wind is blowing. The smile is the same.

Outside

H E STOOD AT THE WINDOW and remembered the
outside as if that were his house and this warm
place, the tousled ruffled presences her hands had left in
the folds of drapes by pulling them open then later (how
much later, how much seen and how much turned from)
pulling them closed, this place where porcelain cups propose the unlikeliest destinations, were in fact the whole
world. Inside is outside and he is lost.

To be lost inside your house is a strange religion. Her
mother's tarot cards are spilled on the drumhead table,
glass over flame mahogany, some face up—that is the
future—and some face down—that is the future that will
never come to be his, somebody else's future, the kind
a lover maybe has in mind when he turns to the one he
loves and says Share my future with me, his voice weak-

ens, some of it at least, she looks at his hands as he's talking, blue veins and red muscle, how simply we are made, all futures are the same, she thinks, we are in the same room, same wind, same seeds, same answers. She doesn't have to say anything to him because already he doesn't understand. To say anything would mean he would understand even less.

Or maybe that is best, she thinks: Understand nothing, and then we are free. Free to begin. She shrugs a silky cardigan off her shoulders and slips it onto a plastic hanger, holds it over the left index finger like a fish she's caught in the air, sly, supple, quivering. There is a stone that means this kind of light, halfway between stone and silk, between a fish and a man. She looks up at her grandmother's crucifix on the wall beside the dried yellow roses. On the dead man's ivory body a little gouge of wound had been filled years ago with some red pigment to stand for blood. Now a strange thrill goes through her as she sees the lips of the wound are kissed with dust, the dust of this room, her dust stuck to god's wound.

The man is still looking out the window, his hand resting on the pane as if he wanted to become glass. In fact she can seem to see light coming through the thin skin of his fingers, that crimson light that children learn when they play with flashlights, the light of the inside of the body. Our real color. The one we all are truly, the color inside. Sacred crimson. What is the name of the stone we are supposed to become?

The Yoke

HERE WAS A MAN who began to invent hour by hour
the outlines, shadows, details of another world. It began as a what-if kind of fantasy, but little by little he found
himself spending more and more of his mental time in
that imagined reality. As he built that world, his purchase
on this world we share with him began to slip. Or not
so much slip as to seem first relative, then arbitrary, finally indifferent. Though he had never been interested in
economics or politics, in that other world (that World of
Mine he called it for a long time, before he discovered its
proper name) he took great pains to supervise constantly
the market trends, banking systems, the structures of
power. Our man began to lose interest in this shared
world of ours. Nothing bad happened to him—he could
still drive a car, stop at red lights, cash his paycheck, get to

work more or less on time. But the veil was trembling all the time, and the wind from elsewhere drove him. It drove him gently, always gently, deeper into reality, that reality, the interest rates, hydroelectric projects, space program, postage stamps, cathedrals of his other world. He composed its dictionaries, outlined its history, saw from the hilltop of his mind the bloodiest of its ancient battles, the triumphs of its modern technology, its more than modern justice, social equity, compassion.

In our world, he stopped going to work, stopped staying in his house. He began to move along the roads, walking, sleeping here and there, eating what he found. Such a life, though rough and occasionally subject to bewildering affronts from subjects who did not seem to recognize him, pleased him. He was the sort of king who was not haughty; he roamed like Aaron the Just through Baghdad incognito, seeing how the Law was maintained. He was the sort of king who held the Law above all other things, grew it in his heart, spread it out from his empty hands as he walked the roads of our silly, half-baked world. It was important for him to arrange for the continuation of his just rule, the installation of a dynasty founded on truth and justice. He had just welcomed his first-born son's maturity in that world, had just presided over the solemn conclave in which all the nobles, heiresses, witches and cardinals of his realm had participated, swearing oaths of fealty to his son and presumptive heir. So it was with satisfaction and contentment that, at the same hour, he accepted the solicitations of death in this world. He lay down in a gully beside the highway outside Albany and pondered the rich fulfillment of his life's work.

Thinking of this man's exemplary life, I realize that the

dream I am currently sharing with you, and the whole terrain—language, book, chair, table, landscape, sacred incident light—we share that makes all our other sharings possible, is of course only one among many dreams. Our successes in this life are achieved at the expense of our selves in some other life. I urge you not to forget, not even for a day, these other selves of ours. In like manner I must keep in mind the one of me who even now, as I am looking with satisfaction at the shapely completion of this paragraph, is dying poor and shivering but content, in a world not so far away, and in fact has just this instant died.

The Geese in December

———————⊱•◦•⊰———————

HONKING IN AQUA SKY. Look up here to meet us, a wedge of geese. A vee for you. Low we come from the dull east into sunset. Twenty-nine, thirty of us. It's hard for you to be certain of our number. Watch. Vreik on the lower arm of our vee swims over to the upper, then two sisters dropped out of that and fell back to our lower, then three from the far end end of the trail behind me fell into the middle of our vee and accelerated. Now our form slows to engulf them in their new places. This is our Shift. We are a slow subtle changing in the sky. We go on changing as long as we fly.

I am the one on the right, the front, that sometimes edges out even in front of the front, and am the point, and fall back and am the slope, and all the while I don't have to bother being me, since all I am is where I am.

What we do we do for our delight. It is our sheer play, complex patterns and series (like your bell-ringers ringing changes) developing for the sheer joy of the play. We ring bells in emptiness. No one can hear them, but down below they can hear us. We cry as we play, our dance falls down upon the world like a single cry heard.

We play, and it is our religion and our art. It is what down there they would call poetry or music, not like sport. We are singing and carving and speaking with our accelerations and retardations, our left wing and right wing, our whole vee is our great momentary self, our Us, in which each little one of us plays a part. From this play we find identity and delight. Simple it is and clear, we do happiness in this silver street the sky, we do our dance and we cry, and when we have to we come down.

This is what Vreik was saying by his first move to the forward right, and we move with him to say the rest of it. All we're doing is saying. Down there some people saw up and wrote down in dust or on paper what they saw. They copy our Forms, but they turn our fluent never-stopping changes into fixed patterns, their alphabet we were. But we are always beyond what they could write down, or even what they could say. We never fix in one pattern, so we are beyond language too.

And on the other side of language there is only song. Or do I mean dance. Song and dance. What we do. Whatever we do. We think there will never be an end to this Form, a Form that changes and changes, and we form as long as we fly. Sometimes we have to come down to eat and sleep. But always the morning returns us to ourselves, returns us to the figure of the dance.

This is our happiness and art—evolving and abandoning patterns in the sky. Stars do this too, but do it slow. We are faster, restless, serene. It takes great effort to fly, I wonder if you know that down there. We think you think we do it without toil. Not so, it is song and dance and hard to do, and the wind helps us, and the little drops of water that make cloud and rainbow and sundogs and all the other things we choose to move through. But it is hard to do. Happiness is hard.

Do you have happiness? Do you have a Form? Do you have a Form in which you move all the days of your life, until you rest peacefully at night floating on that not very playful surface of the ground you like so well? We rest on water, which is always moving. And when we're quiet on land we're there to dream, and our dreams then are movement enough for us.

But you? Tell us someday, somehow, of the Form you move and make. We look down sometimes, not long enough to get distracted from the grace of our Form, but we don't understand your Form yet. Help us to understand how and what you do. Is it building things and leaving them there? Is it moving all alone on roads?

We have been doing what we do a long time, so our art is very perfect in its pure availability. Just look at us, just watch us move. All ancient arts make it easy for you. Hard as it is for us, we give it to you.

A Simple Room

F OR MANY YEARS, the admirably placed and interest-
ingly furnished chalet of Madame Gallay has been
the envy of all the housewives of the hamlet of La Borne,
in the old Duchy of Savoie, on the left bank of the river
Dranse one hears all night rushing down from the high
massifs to the south. The chalet is called "Les Mouflons,"
and its owners run a successful crêperie in the ski and
parapente town of Les Gets up the valley and over the
mountain. Their restaurant is called by a word that means
Jackdaw in English, Kafka in Czech, while here it also
has the local meaning of the heroic fighters of the Resistance who were so active, and so successful, in this part of
France. The name of the chalet, though, just means those
mountain goats seldom seen these days in the hills below
the Roc d'Enfer.

The largest room in the chalet is rich with its considerable population of what used to be called objects of virtue —objects decorative, sentimental or puzzling that occupy many of the flat surfaces of the room, most of all the broad sills of the clerestory windows. Objects anywhere in the world always seem to draw the viewer into some intrigue, and these do so more than most.

Where the staircase turns, on its way to the balcony that overhangs the room, the wall is ornamented with a large cluster of grapes, huge, in polished wood, complete with wooden grape leaf and wooden trucial coil. The grapes are of various sizes, the largest five inches or so in diameter, the smallest no more than two inches. A visitor seated at the dining room table, left alone for a moment, might amuse himself by counting the grapes, and would find their total to be sixteen in the big cluster. This imposing arrangement, high on the roughcast wall, is the most elevated object in the room, not counting the two wagon wheels, still iron-felloed, which hang down from the transverse beams. Each is fitted at the hub, in lieu of an axle, with a spotlight, sunken, that beams its light straight down.

Under the wooden grapes, on the curve of the stairs, a china elephant, much smaller than life-size, stands, its howdah is a pedestal. Remarkably, nothing stands on this. North of the elephant is a tall grandfather clock stopped at 5:56. On the case of the clock, a decal shows flowers of the hydrangea or hortensia sort. Below this is a candelabra with four metal candles rising out of the base of white gardenias, false as the candles. Under the large, sloping window, which from some angles shows La Grande Terche, 'the big cliff,' and which at night is bright with the streetlight over the roadsign that marks the place as

La Borne, 'the boundary,' is a broad, tall china cabinet. On top of this, we are reading from south to north, are two wooden tub-like objects meant to hang on the wall, perhaps to uplift flowers. Certainly the wooden souvenir-like objects are decorated with decals of flowers. Next, to the south, is a blue kerosene lamp; an oval basket of artificial flowers, one of which looks vaguely like a peony improbably arisen from autumn foliage. North of that, a tall kerosene lamp in celadon green. Then a wooden butter-mold whose whole function was to intaglio a pretty rose on a loaf of butter. Then a tiny wooden souvenir in the shape of a cottage with thatched roof. Beyond that, at the very edge of the cabinet, a tall object, rectangular, on the fore-edge of which a landscape has been painted; but because the box is on its end, the landscape finds itself running perpendicular to its conventional situation.

Beyond the china closet, the floor bears a four-footed ceramic, green-slipped flower-stand, three feet tall, supporting a Grecian-style, garlanded flower-pot of the same material as the base; from it a very dry dracena-like plant, size of a small tree, rises high along the wall, reaching and almost obscuring a flat panel bearing the outline of a clock stopped at 9:23. The rough-cast wall now meets the wooden upper wall of the chalet on the south side. A ledge runs beneath the large window on either side of the central chimney. Starting at the right, a panel bearing the outline of two ducks, or perhaps swans, long-necked ducks or short-necked swans; the outline of these animals is formed by what, from down below (we are looking at them up there, ten feet above our floor), looks like dried bits of feather that have been used to outline the birds with their red beaks on a brown wooden background.

Past the ducks are: a brown and amber-slip pitcher, a mauve-and-white-slip pitcher, a milk pitcher displaying a decal of a cow, a blue pitcher with an edelweiss, a green pitcher with Grecian festoon, a blue pitcher with a five-petalled flower in red, a pale-blue pitcher with pale-blue flower in white, a brown jug with Grecian festoon, a beige-colored jug with a sunflower, a very large jug with a pattern of flowers (white and green in the reddish glaze), a very large two-handled pottery canister holding perhaps two gallons, dark brown, with another of the same in a paler brown. This gives way to the elaborate stone chimney-piece, on which, about eight feet above the floor, is hung an elaborately ornamented clock, whose antique face bearing roman numerals insists that the time is two minutes after one. Below this on the chimney-face are two copper plates; one of them, with its inside facing us, shows a determined woodsman with a large axe about to chop at a tree-stump tall as himself. The angle of his arms is such that he will never succeed in striking this trunk, so his image facing us, green tree in the background, must express a perpetual dissatisfaction with the geometry of everyday life. Across from this, a copper pan with two handles, its bottom facing us, shows in relief a baker removing a baked loaf from his oven, in front of which stands a basket with an assortment of breads in it, brown and long. Between these two copper objects, but closer to the second, a hexagonal child's beadwork of a jack-o-lantern, smiling, made in plastic beads. Just past the chimney is another tree in a large green pot, standing actually on the apron of the chimney. The tree, not easy to identify, has lance-shaped leaves in dark and bright green mottled. Round the slim trunk, an ivy-like vine has chosen to grow.

Above the tree on the window-ledge, balancing the jugs and pitchers on the other side: a woodsaw in its wooden case; a pale pine tube from which three hand-carved wooden tulips, brightly painted red, emerge; against the sky, an antique mallet, upside down, looks like the hammer of Thor, fallen. Next to it, another agricultural implement of elusive purpose leans against the mullion of the window. It has two handles, a trough in the middle from which a tongue-like piece of wood emerges; handle slits are on either side. There are old people in the town who will certainly know what it is. Beside it, teeth against the window, the head of an antique hay-rake. Beside it, twenty-four sharp teeth pointing upward, is what looks like a carding-frame. Beside this, an ornamental bellows, nozzle down, ornamented with white flowers. Then a perfectly functional ordinary kerosene hurricane lamp. A grocer's scales, each pan eight inches broad. Another wood-saw leans against the rafter just where it joins the outer wall. Under the angle of the saw, a wooden basket, apparently empty, stands directly below the rafter. Next to it, an old wooden scoop in which someone could lift two pounds of flour at a try. Beside it, a two-man draw-saw stands sideways, still with its blade attached.

Now to the eastern window: on the ledge before the eastern window, the decor shifts to the culinary. Four hand-cranked coffee grinders lead the way north. The first, green rectangular, the second white rectangular and decorated in a belle-époque fashion, the third wooden and typical of those used still in New England, with a little drawer in the front into which the ground coffee falls. The fourth is wooden of a kind unfamiliar to me. All four are used by cranking the handle sideways horizontally. After the coffee-grinders proceed five coffee pots, the first with a pointed spout looking like camping gear; the next four, far prettier, with curved spouts and ornate handles and decorated lids. All four point in the same direction, like elephants on parade, their spouts raised to, as if praying to, a vast antique espresso maker, three feet tall, topped with a gilded swan, just where in Italy one would expect to find an eagle. This espresso machine stands in front of the wide wooden mullion that separates the two halves of the window. Beyond the espresso maker are four more vessels, the first a very large cafe-filtre with spout again pointing to its source machine; then a conventional ewer, graceful enough but having no explicit reference to coffee, has somehow inserted itself in this parade of coffee pots. It is followed by two completely appropriate, decorated nineteenth-century cafe-filtre pots in porcelain. Beneath these pots, a two-barreled shotgun is mounted, with its carrying strap. Its barrels point past a wooden hanging basket of artificial flowers and a large platter bearing an improbably recent painting of two ancient Greek warriors confronting each other, towards an immense white goose, larger than life-size, in bright china, with a very yellow bill, and black shiny eyes. This stands on a lowboy, its upraised tail propped against a framed tapestry of a heart outlined by many little hearts surrounding an indecipherable flower above which "Bienvenue" has been embroidered in blood-red. The goose wears a black ceramic kerchief, and someone has slipped over goose head and neck, so that it lies on the goose's broad shoulders, a silk ribbon in grosgrain. Below the goose's right shoulder, a picture frame shows three cherubs, the middle one resting its cheek on its hand, the one on the right blowing a kiss to the viewer over its left palm, the one on the left with its right palm. These three cherubs are perched on top of a small looks-to-be handmade frame inside which two pictures are displayed, one of them a North African merchant squatting in front of his stall where huge piles of pepper, cumin, and other spices are colorfully arrayed; in front of him is a grocer's scale exactly like the much older actual one that faces the picture from across the room. Below the photo of the spicer and his wares is a picture of a crowd in Marrakech; in the foreground three French women admire a camel seated before them. The woman on the left pats the camel's head with her right hand. A child between the first and second woman gazes diffidently at the camel. Another child in Basque jersey, safe between the second and third woman, nevertheless hides his head between the women as if in fear of the camel. To the left of this interesting picture, under the shoulder and by the immense yellow foot of the china goose, a small, dingy papier-mâché duck is sitting, looking up in terror at the goose; or it might just be hiding behind the goose from the shotgun that is still aimed at all these exhibits. Behind the duck sits a small pottery chicken, or better rooster. It says on the bottom: "Poule ou coq." Coq, however, is misspelt cog next to the mutilated bar-code indicating that this object cost someone 25 francs, or in smaller print, 3.81 Euros—the ambiguous pricing argues the fairly recent acquisition of this ambiguous fowl. Next to the rooster or chicken's right wing is the large wooden bowl that is found in every bar and tourist attraction in the Savoy, the large wooden vessel used to mix and drink from that ceremonial wassail, *la Grolle*. It is round and flat, the top carved roughly in floral pattern lifts off, and in the roughly two-quart interior, la grolle is mixed. From four spouts, crosswise disposed, friends, strangers and travelers can all drink from the same vessel. By tradition, the whole vessel, spouts and all, must be carved from a single piece of wood. Past *la grolle*, and directly in line with the beak of the goose who seems to examine it with speculation, stands an enigmatic and perplexing object. It is a plastic flower, size of a softball, made up of tiny plastic flowers in bright green, studded here and there with bright red currants, also plastic. The whole stands on a thick green stalk and comes out of a perfectly ordinary flower-pot. Beside it, however, arises a green plastic sheaf of wheat, as if displaced from some lost Eleusinian ceremony. Both the strange green plastic flower made up of many flowers and the fugitive plastic sheaf of wheat stand out of a cluster of plastic, bright-red snapdragon-like flowers.

Moving east from this enigma, we see against the side of the lowboy a tall warming-pan with a three-foot handle. The pan's lid is embossed with the fierce round bearded face of the Sun, looking quite Old Gaulish.

At or slightly above eye-height, around the room, are pictures and paintings. First, on the north wall, beside the stair, in a rustic wooden frame, mortise and tenon constructed, three printed photographs labeled "Les Alpes." These three photographs show: the top of the Matterhorn, or something like it; the roof of a chalet drowned in snow, with snow-bearing pines behind it; an alpine meadow seen through a screen of pink epilobes. The wide frame is wreathed with a length of rope, twig, and stem into which have been worked pine cones, leaves, and less nameable arboreal evidences.

On the south wall, under the clerestory windows, beginning under the swans and pitchers, we encounter the first of seven oil-paintings, all by the same hand. Three are in the shape of tombstones, for some reason. The first shows a nineteenth-century couple leaving footprints as they walk through the snow towards a Savoyard village covered in snow, big flakes of snow still falling; the second is an autumn scene, haystacks, bare trees, a church steeple, a snow-covered mountain, some vigorous fir trees. The third brings us back to winter again. Houses, a low wall, a muffled figure facing tracks it has already left in the snow and has now whirled round to check the size of his progress. The houses in the middle distance have blue shutters. Snow covers all. The fourth picture has for some reason been removed from its position on the ledge and is leaning against the fireplace. It shows a lake in summer, filling up the lower half of the tombstone; beyond it, a very tall church steeple over red house roofs. Behind that in turn are sharp peaks of those low mountains that elsewhere in France are called "alpilles." A hawk is soaring towards a storm-cloud. Behind the storm, the radiance of what might be a daytime moon. It is not clear why this pleasant image, amateurish though it is like all the rest, has been demoted from the picture-rail to stand, almost unseeable, in the chimney-corner, half-hidden by a terrestrial globe inscribed in French. There is still a Soviet Union; there is still a Rhodesia. Behind the globe, a teddy-bear made of straw stands with its nose pressed against the side of the TV. A child who picked it up with the enthusiasm teddy bears deserve might be roughly scratched. Behind the bear stands a pewter lantern with a candle lying toppled in it. Above this bear's nose, and perched on top of the television set, is a bright Russian doll with a painted pink face and little cupiedoll lips. It is the sort of doll that usually opens up to reveal many smaller dolls just like itself in descending sizes all nested within. This one however, when opened, reveals the tip of a brush, a yellow wax crayon, a small pencil-sharpener, and the stub of a violet pencil for it to sharpen. There is also a tiny red gingham bow. Past the television set is another straw, bear-like creature, this one looking even less caressable than the first. Then a small table bearing the radio tuner, the VCR and its gear. Past that, still in the entertainment corner, there sits on the very rim of the tile ledge a metal wavy-lipped tray filled with artificial flowers in the midst of which a round, green candle, partly burned, sits in an angle. In front of this, a big stone owl with a gold ribbon and cord around its neck faces into the room. The ribbon is bright but not as bright as the beak of the owl, which gleams in the morning sun.

Right next to the fireplace itself stands a metal pot full of artificial flowers.

In front of the window on the southeast, in a child's cradle (perhaps replica, perhaps original) of the late nineteenth century, the infant's place is taken by two potted plants, one a sort of dracena or snakeplant, and one the sort playfully called mother-in-law's tongue. In the southeast corner of the room, next to these plants, stands a wooden barstool, with bent wood buttressing. This supports a very large Christmas cactus, not in flower. This four-foot-wide cactus partially hides a curio cabinet, which stands right beside the east window in this southeast corner of the room. The cabinet has four shelves. On the first shelf, at the top, above eye level, a pewter candleholder with one half-melted candle; a green glass apothecary jar with gilt decoration. A strange figure, perhaps it is a bottle, in the form of a grey female creature in grey robe holds what seems like a small infant, also in grey. She might be a nun, or an ancient noblewoman, or a nightmare figure that comes to snatch children away, a Lilith of the mountains. Her face is perfectly heart-shaped, cream-colored against the grey of her wimple and robe. She has a small mouth, and her eyes have no pupils. Standing beside her, sitting upright in the begging posture, is a dog with a very long neck, china, with brightly colored flowers dotted here and there about its body and paws.

On the second shelf at the left is another candle-holder, this one in brightly-colored clay, made presumably by a child. Next to it, a small ointment jar has "Rebecca" written on it. Beside it, a small black tea caddy from Jackson's of Piccadilly, full of stones. Next to it, a small ointment pot, with two infants in clay in ceramic on top of it. You open it by pulling up the infants. Next to the infants, and actually resting on the head of the girl infant, is the spout of an ornamental and impractical teapot that would hold perhaps a cup of tea. Alongside it is a china shoe, empty, shaped for the right foot of an infant. The china shoe has a cloth ribbon and plastic flowers attached where the laces would be.

On the third shelf, a glass yogurt jar has been wrapped in paper. On it, a childish hand has written in crayon, "Mamie bonne fête." In front of this, a small china dog sports with its puppies. Something sad happens then: a young china gentleman, seven inches tall, dressed in eighteenth-century costume, has lost his right hand. Worse than that, his head was broken quite off on the line running through the lower jar of the right to the upper jar of the left, and it has been mended, not unskillfully, so the boy can still look out with the serene smile common to china figurines. Next to him and partly hanging over him is a floral vase containing a pint, but not of liquid; containing instead an assortment of unusual festive characters: two one-horned devils, for example; a large bumblebee; a parrot with blue and yellow feathers and red bill; all of these made from pipecleaners. Then a larger creature with three snaky heads, two large creatures, perhaps serpents, serpents made from some pipe cleaner-like material that winds around tall plastic stalks upright in the jar. Almost hidden inside the jar is a dragonfly in plastic with pipecleaner obbligato and sticking out of the jar too is a perfectly ordinary Guatemalan wooden brightly painted gift-shop parrot. The snakes are yellow and have long red tongues. Beside this, a small étui of wood carries an embroidered cover showing an auk-like bird perched in flowers.

On the fourth shelf is a copper cauldron, a miniature version of the kind that, full size, hang from the ledges of this and many another alpine chalet. This little one supports a candle or candle-like object coated in gold metal. Beside it, another plate of the woodsman chopping a tree his blade cannot reach stands beside a small goat bell, perhaps the most beautiful object in the room, made of bell metal with an iron strap atop it, marked on the metal primitively with a sun and a moon. In the corner of the lowest shelf in the cabinet stands a wooden cuckoo clock, non-functioning, both in respect of the time it does not keep and the cuckoo it does not emit. It does, though, have the shape of an alpine chalet, a stylized and somewhat more folkloric version of the building in which all this has been collected and displayed. Before the tiny, romantic chalet stands a cutout figure of a green fir tree in front of which in turn is an improbably large bright red white spotted amanita mushroom. Over the clock proper, a bluebird seems to have been snared on the ledge of the chalet.

But there is a real cuckoo clock in the room. It hangs beneath the wooden mallet of Thor right next to the chimney piece, on the south wall of the chalet, below the window through which one can see the top of La Frasse, a curiously conical mountain of twelve hundred meters just south of town. The cuckoo clock, though, is a misnomer: it is not a cuckoo clock, it is rather a clock of the German style in which peasant figures are meant to come out and pass before the eye as the hour strikes, as their little turntable admits them, displays them, and conceals them in turn. The clock itself says it is 8:24. On either side of the clock beaks up towards the figure are two figures that might be birds or might be floral. They seem to have beaks, but their colors are those of no birds that live in Germany or Switzerland. Next to this clock is an oval painting by the same hand as all the others. It shows two shacks in the mountains, again in winter, with a rickety fence not quite connecting one with the other. Before the door of each shack or cabin are signs of a path. Each cabin has a chimney. Each chimney is emitting dense black smoke, as if a month's worth of newspapers were being burnt inside. To the east of this is another painting, oddly shaped: imagine a tombstone with two rectangulars on either side of it, or perhaps a bay window. Here is a long street covered in snow spottily bordered on one side by a tall grey wall; along the street a man with an umbrella furled is walking slowly behind his dog. They are on their way to the heart of the village, where a number of buildings cluster around a low-steepled church. A fenced field is at the left side of the road.

In the corner is another oval showing a figure muffled in heavy clothing; the figure wears a tall hat, and leaves tracks in the snow as he or she advances up a road between a granary and two chalets towards a fence beyond which is a church that looks very much like our own little church in La Moussière, 'the mossy place.'

On the east wall in the same corner is a framed reproduction of a painting of a large, handsome building of the nineteenth century with hills beyond it. It is not labeled, but it could very well be the *établissements thermales* down in Thonon-les-Bains, where one can take the waters, or be immersed in greenish healing mud. Beside the painting is a black and white photograph of mountain barns and sheds with snow mountains behind them, with a cherry tree in the foreground, not in blossom. This photograph has been mounted on cardboard and is unframed. Next to it, in an entirely different style, is a framed painting or reproduction, a gouache in full naive style showing scenes of peasant life. A woodcarver is carving a life-size figure of a saint or wanderer. Near him at work is a heart-shaped pond. A house is being built, tiny workmen imposing the roof beam. In the middle distance, a building with turreted roof proclaims itself a MENUISERIE. Beyond this wood-working plant is a pond with a sawmill, and quite a big truck loaded with logs is driving towards it. Beyond the roof of the sawmill many large logs have been piled up neatly. Beyond that, a modern backhoe is lifting some logs from the ground. Not far away a small house has tiny cows in its front yard. Beyond all that, hills and mountains. All the proportions seem studiedly wrong; large and small give no information about near or far. This picture hangs directly below the large espresso maker. Beyond the window, to the left and thus on the northeast corner of the room, just before the goose and just under the muzzle of the shotgun, mounted against the wooden wall above the light switch are first of all: a child's drawing of perhaps a dog mounted sideways so that it looks more abstract and perhaps more interesting than it is. Below that is a large thermometer registering both Fahrenheit and Celsius; at the moment it reads 21°C (71°F). Above the column of mercury is a large raised relief of a goose looking backwards over its tail towards a farm in the distance. Yet another goose in raised relief (small plaster, glued to the back) just beyond it has lost its head and is available to the viewer only as a large white irregular object with a pointed wing. Below the thermometer is a large hard-to-see child's picture, as if birthday cake for a five-year-old, though the number 6 is plainly written on it. Underneath, a card shows a penguin wrapped warm in muffler and tall hat carrying in his left flipper a wrapped parcel—he is wishing the occupants of the room *Bonne année* and *meilleures voeux*. Beneath the light switch, and jammed into the doorframe, a small cloth figure of another penguin has been wedged.

At the center of the room stands a fig tree, Ficus benjamina, in a large green ceramic tub. In the branches of the tree are: a bodyless snowman, wearing blue hat, muffler, and mittens on his no arms; a cluster of plastic raspberries hanging from a high branch; another cluster of plastic raspberries hanging a little lower down on the other side of the tree. On the branch furthest to the south (that is, in the direction of Mont Blanc) a little cloth sheep wearing a pale green jumper hangs by its head. Straight across from it, at the highest point of the tree, just past the first cluster of false raspberries, a gold ribbon in plastic has been hung loosely, forming a kind of double helix dangling from the topmost leaf. In the very center of the tree, in cloth, with blue and avocado wings, perches a bright red parrot. Yellow beak and feet. A bright green eye.

V

The Ritual

Only the poor and the lonely remember
H. P. LOVECRAFT

HE HAD BEEN WALKING for a long time and it was time to finish. He knew why he was walking but not how to do the thing he called finish. Telos. Telestes. Ending things. It was something his mother had told him then pretended she hadn't, whenever he asked about it later. His father always denied it without a word, just looked away out the window. What pale eyes a father has! How far away they see! How they never face anything that is here. Years ago he had started walking, to get away from the place his father refused to look at, him, there, wherever he was, and reach that other place that his father was looking at always. Reach that place and do something there. What was he supposed to do? Maybe he would know when he got there. Build something, kill something, break something, say something—there are

so few things we know how to do, really. From what his
mother said then denied, from what his father never said
but always watched, empty-hearted, far, he had tried to
piece together instructions for his life. What should he
do. What should anyone do. So he walked there, wherever it was that he would know by this fact alone: that he
would stop there and go no further. Somehow he knew he
would know when to stop. Or know that he had stopped,
and notice only then, and it would be right. Meantime,
everybody who looked away from him was looking there.
He just had to follow their empty glances, their embarrassed or irritated lookings-away, and he would know the
way. And somehow his body would know when to stop.
Then he knew he would take something out of his pocket
and use it. Or else pick something off the ground, right
there in the street or on the beach, and use it. And he
would know how to use this thing, and what other thing
or things to use with it, and what rhythm to use in playing
one thing against the other. He would know the words to
say. He is sure that at that moment he will listen to the
inside of his head and hear some words, and all he'll have
to do is say them out loud. And it will be done.

Letter to Thomas Bernhard

———————

I DON'T KNOW WHY I'M bothering to write to you. You're dead, for one thing. All we really share is a love for Glenn Gould and long sentences, probably that's the same love in different forms. Forms of art. I think it's mostly because I want to borrow your complaining tone. Really, your skill at complaining and making the reader keep reading, even liking, the diet of groans, the antiphonal maledictions of your characters. Such skill, skill indeed. But *immer schimpfend*, said a woman in Vienna years ago when I said I liked your work, she didn't like it, you were always bitching. Maybe some other word, meaning to complain and to blame, at once. I have a lot to complain about, and who else can be trusted to listen but a dead man, a man what's more who in some sense chose to be a dead man at this very time when I need a living

man, a man four years older than I am, in fact, no older
than my first wife, a woman who died the same year that
you died, if my facts are straight, they seldom are. Dead
man, will you be my friend? Or at least listen, that's the
least you can do. Maybe even the most, but I can't say.
What do I know about the dead? It's the living, of course,
I suppose, that are the problem. The living, and the way
we set about to be living. For one thing, the most terrible
thing of all probably, I hate grown-ups. I have hated
grown-ups all my life, I hate grown-ups and now I have
become one. Isn't that horrible? The way Saul woke up
and found he was himself a hated Christian. Only no toppling swoons and flashing lights for me, just the slow in-
exorable Work of the Mirror that paints time's grisaille on
my cheekbones, time's sly etching technique using no
mordant fiercer than the nervous hours. What can I do? I
hate grown-ups, the way I hate nature. Nature will kill
you every time. As you know perfectly well, I'm just re-
minding us both, from nature there's no way out but out.
I hate grown-ups and I look just like a grown-up, who
would know the truth looking at me? The way you
changed in your television interviews, from the smooth
cheeked shy author of the late 1960s to the blotched skin
and annoyed celebrity, almost arrogant, of the late interviews, but who can blame you, such dumb questions,
your books said it all, what did they want you to say that
language had not already told them? You looked like a
man in bad health in those last interviews, and so you
were, and sure enough you came to die. Stories are told
about that but I'm not interested in stories. Not now. Before, you were alive; after, you were dead. And what ac-
cesses of choice or refusing to choose, of will or negation

of will, may have come between those two states, that's
not on my mind now. You did what you had to do. Bless
you, my heart goes out to you, glad to have heard you, a
little, glad to have read you. You did me good. What I can
do for you is another matter. Nothing, I suppose. Though
we both come from people who believed, or said they believed, in praying for the departed souls, the souls in Pur-
gatory, praying for them, their happiness in whatever follows life, does anything, doesn't matter, praying for them
is at least praying for other people, that can't be wrong,
can it? Can't hurt might help we say. Yet selfishly we pray
for *our dead*, our own departed. And what about all the
billions unknown to us, nameless to us, not *our* dead at
all, not ours at all except by species, if even that. But at
least we pray. So this letter is a little bit praying for you,
you who are off in some condition that likely is wholly
imaginary, in the course of a survival that is to say the least
problematic, and which, if it has any currency at all, that
is to say, if it exists, is likely to be of a sort splendidly (or
glumly) impersonal. You survive the way the world sur-
vives. You survive in me. Any me, of course, not this particular grieving animal who addresses you now, you would
have put that in italics so I will, this *grieving animal who
speaks to you now.* Am I trying to flatter you by writing like
you, a little, not that I could really write like you, your
gravitas, humor, skill, charm, rhythm, but I *can certainly
seem to be trying to*—is that flattery, or mockery? No para-
graphs, no quotations marks, no let up till the end, just
like you know what. What we've been talking about all
along. And whereas this business of death—almost a commercial concern, Death, Inc.—for the sake of which life
seems to be conducted, Death as the exclusive beneficiary

of all our sweat and so forth, fluid after fluid, has preoc-
cupied writers of every kind from before the beginning of
the alphabet to this day, it is not death that is the problem
here, the one I entered into this (dreary as it must be for
you) correspondence to examine and deplore. No, it is in
fact birth. Birth is hard. It is degrading. I am complaining
about birth. Not, as usual with so many of us, complaining, blaming, *schimpfen*, about being born. No, being here
is fine. Or ineradicably as it is, no question. No question
about being here makes sense. But having to get born to
get here, that's just wrong. The fact that for thousands of
years, as they say, since the ice, we have been being born
from inside someone else's body. What a humiliation!
What a degradation of the woman, of the child. This is
intolerable. It is time to change it. The fact that we have
accepted this state of affairs, this outrageous, post-Edenic
way of making more of us is the worst of all our practices,
and not doing anything to change it is the worst failure of
human imagination and skill since we let Atlantis founder.
That we worm our way out of the flesh, are born like mag-
gots, soft and defenseless and foul-smelling and bedewed
with our mother's agony, this is not how it should be. This
is not art. This is not science. This is not culture. This
must change. Don't ask me how. How isn't your business,
not any more, and certainly not mine. I have certain pictures of my own in my head, about how that change
might look if it did happen. Pictures of pale chambers lit
by an eternal unnatural light, like the magic caverns of
Damanhur or the crystalline abysses in the Mines of Fa-
lun. In these places there would be wandering about, and
from these chambers, caves, grottoes of the future, there
would come quiet happy grown-ups full of kindness and

wisdom, yes, there could be such beings in the time to come, grown-ups wandering, wandering purposefully through the luminous *definition*, watering and tending and pruning and whispering little fairy-godmother spells of pure DNA. Intentional. Carefully thought-out. Tender. Humming a new song for new cells. They would coax one another into being, new being. By chemicals and word of mouth we would grow, lit by a curious light spilling out of the mind itself, amplified unnaturally by some bizarre disposition of crystals, think Novalis: *In crystal grottos revelled a luxuriant folk.* They move, we move, in a light in which we would grow each other. I hear in my surmise some of Blake's raving against the rational. Nature is the most rational of all, all of 'her' escapades have rational purpose and foundation. Nature is the enemy, here. Nature is the enemy. Not Novalis's sense of it as our mind in luminous nexus with everything there is, growing and being grown at once. No. Nature as it is understood by the austere simpletons who use the word as their supreme accolade, natural life style, natural food, natural childbirth. I hate nature. Nature is what happens to us, you know that, and what happens to us is what we must despise. If we have anything pure at all, it is our will, maybe, our will to be better and. And. And what. Something beyond nature. I hate nature. *Nature is my Austria.* So it is time for a poetry of pure flesh, or, if that sounds too poetic, for a flesh healed by poetry, flensed of its penchant for begetting, its tendency to swell up inside victim-women its new identities, alien arrivers. These beings who purport to come from our testicles and ova, who demonstrably ripen in our wombs, who are they? Children are horrible, I've always hated them, hated to be around other children when I was a child, hated them even more than I hated adults, but I knew that adults were incurable, but there might still be some hope for Paul or Raymond or Joan or Miriam, my little friends. No doubt I was wrong, and they're all just grown-ups now, or dead, like you. Who knows where children get to? They are always running out of the house. Sometimes they don't come back. Sometimes when they don't come back they're not dead, like you, or grown up, as I seem to be, but are just gone. Gone as a condition, gone as a state of being all its own. They are not some sort of Rilkean 'early-snatched-away,' not at all, instead they vanished into being who they are. As perhaps I may one day too, and as you probably did. Neither child nor grown-up, not woman and certainly not man. Who are we, Thomas, who are we really? I appeal to you, because of the savor of your elevated, abstruse condition, a condition that is bounded by certainties of all kinds, tell me. I love my country with a corrosive scorn like the tender and detailed hatred you affected towards your Austria, all emotions are one, isn't that finally so, all emotions are just *kleshas*, just ways we feel, habitual energies prompted into doing. Who cares what we feel? A feeling is just something you feel. So what. Call it love, call it hate, I slept almost eight hours last night for the first time in months, and I had no dreams for the first time in weeks. I woke uneasy, knowing *they were up to something*, as it is said, never specifying, never even knowing, who 'they' are. The children, I thought, it might be them, the hated and hate-filled children might be starting at last their long-deferred crusade against the grown-ups and their messed up world. The children, they are detestable, they can't talk, they don't read, they don't love, they don't care about any-

thing that I care about, my poetry and your noble prose
are trash to them, and trash to the adults they are likely to
become. But still I'm on their side, because they march
out, maybe even this very day, with slingshots and tasers
and ninja weapons, against our common enemy, yours
and mine, you called it Austria, I call it Nature, grown-
ups, the president, the pope, the people. Any collective
that has no living beings in it, but only members. A member is a thing incomplete, a hand without an arm, an arm
without a torso, a torso without a man. These children are
still children, alas, not the dream people I foresee and
whose coming into our world, full in flesh but dripping
from no agony, gleaming only with the radiance of the
technology from which they are spoken into the world,
whose coming into the world I demand, demand, no
weaker insistence. Come them into us! Maranatha, new
child! Such raving your silence lets me give vent to, you
who pretend to be dead, how well you hear for a dead
man, you hear like your dead emperors in the Kapuziner-
gruft, I have stood there and heard the banal sanctity of
their anthems, the tumultuous alchemical racket of their
longeval bones, ash, crumble, greasy leftovers of more
than one kingdom stuffed in marble. *At her grave also have
I stood*, you don't need to hear her name yet again. When
I went down those stairs and stood alone among the dead,
why was I alone, where were the tourists who should have
elbowed me aside with their digital cameras, their cold
little *remembering machines*, how had the chill November
rain managed to keep them in their snug buses? I stood
there and listened to the dead, as I listen to you now, and
hear you hearing me, and that Möbius-like infolding of
our hearing lets me talk, it seems, confident of your acous-

tic eternity. If the Hapsburg croakers could hear me, so can you. And you know what I'm asking for, I detest children, so of course I don't want any more of them in the world, but I do want people, people of a sort, of a quality, a limpidity, a torsion, fluid in limb and welcome in fold, people who are born with Bach inside them, children who are never young and adults who are never grown up, these betweeners I yearn for, pretty girls and boys remind us of what they might look like, these yet-to-come, and listening to, say, the Third Partita gives us a sense of what their minds and hearts would be busy with all day long, and quiet at night, and no time for flowers. Flowers are left for the rest of us, we *leftover infantile adults* that the world endures as well as it can, its artists, writers, swindlers, crocodile wranglers, mountain climbers, gardeners, composers of serious modern music. For I would be flesh, and would discourse with my own, and my own have not come into the world. Or they have fled from it, suicided or snatched away by grisly ailments the doctors pretend to name and throw vile-tasting drugs at, or using their radiation and their surgery, grow obscenely rich by maiming those they cannot heal. Someone not born of woman comes to rescue me from my life. I will write again should that person come, or I will come walk with you in the all-too-formal gardens of the afterlife. They may be just like the Schönbrunn you detested, the emperor's palace, his lopsided Versailles with the land's first zoo full of uneasy animals serving life sentences, all of it a pale yellow, color of winter sunlight fading. The name means pretty fountain, doesn't it, or spring, water of the afterlife. When life finally begins.

The Bridge Near Zamorek

THE MALE VOICE SAID: "On the 29th of May, 1904, on the western approaches to the Zamorek Bridge, two cars collided. One, slightly damaged, proceeded on its way to Zamorek without further incident. The other, in which I was, toppled down the embankment into the river, where I drowned. Please read me all the information you can find about this incident, including all the auditorium reports."

I understood the word 'auditorium' as the speaker's mistranslation of a word that means forensic. At the next opportunity, I went to the relevant section of the archives and began assembling the reports requested. As I was lifting the files onto the desk, my telephone rang. An official voice said that a Permissions Command had just been issued by the central office, expressly forbidding all research into the very case with which I was busy at the moment...

At this moment the voice of the archivist ceased.

Edmund Wilson on
Alfred de Musset:
The Dream

———※◦※———

OUTSIDE IT WAS A hot night in Brooklyn while I was busy inside dreaming. This was years ago. The dream started with me reading in the same shabby leather chair I had been sitting in, reading Malory before I went to bed. The chair of course, like everything else, had once been new, really not so long ago. It had been specially made for me at my mother's commission, a red leather club chair, meant for a heavy body reading. After five years of heavy reading, the cushions were penitent, and the sleek scarlet finish was off it. In spots, the smooth red polished leather had worn away, and the rough underpelt showed through.

In the dream, I was reading a book by Edmund Wilson. It was in French, and called *La Vie d'Alfred de Musset*. I was not surprised that Wilson had written it in French. Thomas Mann had written whole passages, mysteries to me, in that language in *The Magic Mountain*. And Wilson himself had used lots of untranslated Russian in his *Memoirs of Hecate County*, a banned book I felt a little queasy about—not like his athletically classic criticism.

But I was a little surprised that I could understand the French. Along went the biography and along went I, reading. Then (this is dream time, the unimportant parts —and who is that Lord of the Dream who passes such unerring judgment over the details of dream?—pass in no time, no time) I turned a page (a page from nowhere —where had I been?) and found myself at the beginning of a new chapter.

This is how it started. (It was printed in French, I was understanding in English.)

At the age of 47, Alfred de Musset learned that he had contracted leprosy.

For years I myself suffered from a strange and terrified leprophobia—the word and its cognates could shock me almost to faintness if I encountered them in casual reading, while even if I knew one was coming, a 'leper' or 'pale victim' could scare me into running about the house and turning lights on, or running into the warm afternoon and hoping for ordinary people. To take away the terrible cold of that word. And even outside, in the Brooklyn nights, the shadows of ailanthus trees and sumac bushes would writhe in the hot wind. They looked tropical and dangerous, rank-smelling trees from Leperland.

It would take a footnote long as life to explain all the plausible meanings and origins of this fear of the words themselves: leprosy, leper, and their relatives. We have no time for that. Dreams need no footnotes but our after-lives, those inferences we experience as days. Dreams are themselves footnotes. But not footnotes to life. Some other transactions they are so busy annotating all night long.

Because of my great fear of leprosy and its words, that opening sentence should have daunted me. But I felt nothing. Just an odd awareness that this time I wasn't frightened.

I read on.

> Do you imagine I'm like the wind of autumn
> That feeds on grieving till it's churchyard time,
> And for whom all pain is just a drop of water?
> O poet, a kiss! I'm the one who kisses you.
> The weeds I wanted to rip up from this place,
> They're just your idleness; your pain is God's.
> Whatever anguishes your youth may endure,
> Let it keep growing vaster, this sacred wound
> The black seraphim made in your heart's core—
> Nothing makes us as great as some great sorrow.

A few weeks ago now, I saw some of these words quoted from Musset in a mystery story I was reading, and grew interested, the black seraphim, the holy wound. And then I remembered my dream of so many years ago.

The dreamed chapter went on. As Edmund Wilson began to describe the first catspaw aggressions of Musset's disease, the pages I was reading began to flicker, and images began to show through the greyish slick cheap paper, the kind Wilson's books were printed on in the late 40s and early 50s (*Classics and Commercials*, for instance, fat squat books.)

The text was dissolving into its story.

The story began to move, until the book, still in my hands, dissolved its pages into a movie I was watching, a movie called *The Life of Alfred de Musset*.

Who are the black seraphim? The French word *séraphin* is used as a singular, though its form is that of the Aramaic or Hebrew plural. In the poem it is *les séraphins*, as if plural of a plural. Who are those so many, many? And what is the *sainte blessure*, the sacred wound?

The movie showed the poet Musset growing ever more reclusive, hardly ever leaving his Paris apartment except by night. Oh it is no small thing to be private, whatever the cost. The loss. Gradually the ravages of his disease, along with a kindly wish not to infect other people, lead him to a brave resolve.

We see him, nicely dressed, stand by the broad low round table in his foyer. The damask tablecloth is neatly littered with reviews and journals. He has had his servants packing for a long journey. His right arm is round the waist of his faithful wife, who smiles at him with a certain sadness. Perhaps it is only wistfulness. They are leaving Paris.

How can one bear to leave, perhaps forever, the capital of the world? Flaubert! Balzac! Berlioz! Wagner will come again. Austria is misbehaving. France of the poets! Manet painted her picture when she was more smiles than she is now, and even so he elicited a somber thoughtfulness in her long features, her good bones.

Now we see them, Alfred and his wife, in an open barouche. They are trotting along in sparkling sunlight by the Mediterranean. They are in Marseilles, about to take ship for French Polynesia.

He looks in the open carriage like a viceroy or a conqueror, all in white and with a Sola topee already natural on his head. But he's just a poet, just a poet with leprosy. He is leaving France forever, and his wife is with him.

As I read, I am aware even in dream that the story I'm

watching, about a poet who in waking life I know noth-
ing at all about, is full of allusions to other stories I do
know: Rémy de Gourmont with his own case of lupus
or leprosy who kept to his rooms in the Rue des Saints-
Pères (to which I went walking, like a pilgrim, in 1954,
just to watch the northern sunlight fall on his long street).
Paul Gauguin eaten up with syphilis (or was it worse?) in
Tahiti. Arthur Rimbaud fleeing to Africa. Fleeing from
Africa to Marseilles. Father Damien beginning his sermon
"We lepers" one bright Sunday morning. Sweet Tusitala,
old Robert Louis Stevenson my father told me all about,
dying in the grass houses of Samoa. But about Musset I
knew nothing. The dream knew, and a dream is not just
invention and creation. A dream is criticism too. Dream
is the theory of the dark.

But the book that was a movie kept going on:

> In his love sublime he cradles all his anguish
> And, gazing down on what pours from his bleeding breast,
> In the midst of this feast of death sinks down and totters,
> Drunk on the senses and tenderness and horror.

Volupté, tendresse, horreur. "...The senses and tenderness
and horror." I like that translation. Who is this, an ocean
or a bird, a father or a lover, who suffers so? It is enough
to understand: someone suffers. Someone undergoes the
long translation of impermanence. The holy wound that
the world gives us feeds the world. We give our blood. All
flesh is fed from ours. The wound works.

In a ship, welcomed courteously and treated like a big
shot, Musset sails with his wife. He is a famous author. No
one knows his ugly medical secret—only his wife and his
doctor, some scrofulous whiskered character back in Paris.
They sail on the broad sweet autumn Mediterranean, away

from Europe. Suez! Everyone wonders why the Mussets do not go ashore at Alexandria, do not visit the Pyramids, the Temple at Luxor, the sands. They do not know that time and sickness are already writing hieroglyphs on him. That is text enough for him to decipher.

Poets! It is enough to read your own skins! There is your narrative and your map of travel. Decode your own bodies, learned critics! Sing your skin while it's still sweet and fresh!

From this point on, the movie follows episodically. The French text by Edmund Wilson has become a persistent English-language voiceover that explains everything we see. We hurry on, to the settlement on some nice French island, tricolor and palm and white schooner in the harbor, polite functionaries from the Civil Service are never far, his wife teaches native children, he gets worse and worse.

His disease thickens in him, until a time comes when even the least observant visitor must recognize that this is a very sick man, with a very serious and disfiguring disease, and most likely an actual leper. Yet all through this time Musset is working. It is the great time of his writing life. From his warped and nerveless fingers come great odes, celebrations of the praises—an island is all praises—of natural fact. Rock, wave, sun, the unforgiving instant twilights of the equator, the impenetrable night below and the dazzling radiance of the southern skies, the svelte haunches of fishermen and their wives, the curious androgyny the ocean works on those who, smooth in sarongs, stand all day long in or near it. The smoothness of skin, the asperity of lemons.

His teeth are going, but he can still suck calmly on sugar cane. He still can smoke the stubby wheat-colored cigarettes his wife rolls for him.

The last scene of the movie is memorable. Ever since the disease started triumphing in him, the camera has been kept upwind of the man's image. We haven't been close. We see him move in the middle distance, and Edmund Wilson's voice tells us what we must understand.

But now at the end the camera ambles up, respectfully slow, to where the great poet—made great by adversity, by his brave dignity in facing it, his transmuted song—sits writing.

Alfred de Musset sits in a roomy wicker chair at a wicker table. His large notebook is open before him, and an ornate early fountain pen is in his left hand. A big cup of tea is nearby, in its saucer. Books are piled handily, and correspondence seems there too, and an ashtray. Alfred is wearing a soft white floppy hat, that shades and thus hides much of his ruined face. He is writing, and then looks up and seems to see us. The changes in shadow beneath the brim of his hat may mean that he is smiling. He speaks. I hear what he says, and see it also, a title on the screen:

"Leprosy is the only suitable condition for the creative artist."

It is the first time since Paris we have heard him speak. He is speaking in English, too, courteous as ever. That shouldn't surprise me—poetry is always courteous. In fact, poetry is the essence of all civility. Every poet answering as best we can, and all day long, the deepest questions the words ask. (The words? The words are us.)

Leprosy is the only condition for the creative artist. It is the wound that isolates him, the nutritious bread of exile, the loss that teaches finding, the dismay that teaches honor for all simple things. When I had the dream, I knew about leprosy and knew, already, a little about exile, though I still was living in the city where I was born. Exile is internal, and ripens inside, the way the sluggish pathogens of leprosy take years sometimes to make their move. To make their mark on their man.

Later, after I woke up, impressed and amused by the dream, and telling it widely, no doubt with illegitimate embellishment, to my circle of acquaintance, I looked up Musset in a reference book and found that the year of his life to which the dream assigned the coming of leprosy was in fact the year of his death. If that's what is meant by fact.

Not long ago, I asked an old friend from the Baltic, who had spent his youth with the Resistance in wartime France, whether he knew about the 'black seraphim' in Musset. He said nothing in his own words, but immediately began reciting the opening alexandrines of "Une Nuit de Mai," which I gather is Musset's big anthology poem, where the Muse cries out (beginning, like an epic, in the middle of some action):

O poet, take up your lute and give me your kiss!

Today I found the text of the poem, and sure enough found towards the end, again in some great sonorous rapture of the Muse of poetry, the lines that haunted me, and brought back after so many years the instructive dream of the sacrifices that are proper to make for the full burgeoning of song. And in the poem, though the poet presumes to speak easily with the Muse, even calling her his sister at one point, in fact the Muse gets all the good lines.

Or rather, strictly, the richness and beauty of all language are in her gift, and she is giving still. Even to the diseased and dying she has a tremendous word to speak. Sweeter than centuries her leper's kiss.

Confessions of Don Juan

SOMEWHERE THERE'S A WIFE who commands him to write. Discovering her identity will take his whole life.

The Confessions of Don Juan are the confessions of Faust.

Don Juan becomes the doctor, Doctor Faust. We suffer from all his degrees. Titles. Names of his novels, operas, plays, poems. Pregnant with fame from the beginning, a smug licentiate. Diplomas rolled, phallic tubes. A bundle of perversions. Speak!

The story of Faust must appear incoherent and tragically chaotic, the way *Faust II* appears at the end of Goethe's life, clarified into marble and gold, daytime and meadow, a radiant perplexity.

There is nothing more seductive than permission: I am permitted. Nothing more seductive than Thou may'st. But not for long.

A window on her sleeping form.

His story must demonstrate how *this* time is as fragmented, unruly, disturbed, as the era of the industrial revolution was—that gave birth to *Faust I*, and that Goethe tried in some curious, copious, way to respond to all through *Faust II* —

or the enterprising merchant-pirate era that saw the first *Faustbuch* and Marlowe's play in a time of exploration, slavery, land-grab as a root of war.

Because Faust always has to be *the* hero of his age, this age.

❧

But his own age: Faust was old to begin with.

Before that, he was Don Juan. And after, again. A cycle. The young libertine ages into the old phallosopher of love, and becomes, just as Plato prophesied, only a philosopher itself. Who then, restless in wisdom, seeks to wield the fist of youth. Reclaim his youth. For, despite the plant that Gilgamesh found and lost, it is not to be young *again* that Faust wants, but to claim his eternal youth. Or, more exactly, eternal adolescence.

Faust is the haughty child-man always seeking *gravitas*, seeking *auctoritas*, seeking *dynameis*, powers, and only 'at the end of the day'

(but the end of his day is Easter morning, when our play or opera begins)

realizing that it is *pulchritudo et voluptas*, beauty and pleasure, that he wanted, we wanted all along.

Only a child could make this mistake, only a child could be healed of his error by falling into the mud puddle and remembering what feeling feels like when it is actually feeling and not thinking about mastery and goal.

Mozart never grew old enough to forget this: Don Giovanni falling down the octave into Hell is the child falling, half-willingly, into the mud puddle.

A child lacks power and authority more than he lacks anything else.

The Will to Power is the will to be Old.

Faust is about Age. Aging. Age in the sense of being old and then not wanting to be the thing you spent your whole life working so hard to become: master, doctor, learned, grave, severe.

And about Age in the sense of epoch, in this age of the world and not another. This age 'of ours' discovered Age as an issue.

❦

There was no Faust before alchemy, no Faust before mercantilism. Banks and trading companies are the direct inventions of alchemy—the transmutation of labor into gold, of paper into gold, of ordinary land into 'owned' land—property—turning landscape into states and boundaries. *Turning experience into commodity*—that is the alchemy housed in Hell's real estate by Dante. But put in charge of the state by Louis XIV and Cromwell alike.

The instruments of power, as of *voluptas*, are infinite.

No end of pleasure, no end of sin, no end of mastery. There is always someone left to subject, to make into a subject, to control. Subjèct: make someone into a serf or monarch's thrall. Sùbject: a mental commodity you study in school: botany or economics.

Goethe's Faust becomes the hegemon of the sea in Part II—powerful old man against the world. Liquidity of money. The colonial moment at its height.

The will to power, like the will to pleasure, is unchanging, an invariant energy, a variable goal. Fatiguing to have to be close to someone who wants. Marguerite does not succumb to her own desires but to his. We faint into the power of another.

Faust wore a business suit in college. He disdained the flute and the guitar. He leaves that to Mephistopheles, to pluck the lute, the apron strings, the delicate tracery of the bra. Stripped bare by mere magic, the woman stands revealed to Faust. Instant nude. The urgency of his own desiring makes him think she's beautiful.

Faust speaks: I will teach you how to be old. Disdain anything that children love. That is enough.

Spend your life secretly yearning for what children have every day.

Dreams of power are commonplace. The will to power (in and out of Nietzsche's sense) is rare.

Heidegger explains that the Will to Power is the Will to Being.

A verb on pilgrimage to the noun. Change of state. Desire's alchemy: to become the thing you desire to possess. The element.

Midas: what he embraces becomes him.

⚜

(thinking about Busoni's opera *Doktor Faust*)

I heard it last night from Berlin, a new production. Take it by ear. It's years since I heard it last, even more years since I last read the libretto. A lot stays in mind though, cries, dreams, passageways, a sly, high devil, a woman in love. To hear music at night is to be an island, thinking.

Wille = 'will,' *Welle* = 'wave.'

There is a dialectic, or certainly a tension, between *Wille* and *Welle*. *Ich, Faust, ein ewiger Wille*, he cries. [I, Faust, an eternal Will!] But also another cry, one I have so many times arising in me, that I have joined with him in making, pompous as it is: *Arbeit, heilende Welle, in dir bad' ich mich rein!* [Work, healing wave, in you I bathe myself pure!]

Work, and the determination to work, and the valuation of work—the word "opera" itself means work—are all prime signifiers in the phallocratic realm. Yet this very

self-important work, this Opus Magnum of the self becoming itself (himself), this archetypal masculine indus-
try, the Work itself, is 'bathed' in a remarkably feminine
image: the wave, the waves. We think of Virginia Woolf's
great novel of lost, shared, found identities, we think of
Undine, of Mörike's *schöne Lau*, Anna Livia Plurabelle
and all the rest of it. So Busoni construes Work as itself
immersion in the woman. Penetration of the wave, yes, to
that extent characteristically virile, but it is the wave that
'does the work,' the healing.

Yet the first time he cries out about the healing wave of
Work, he seems to be abandoning the quest for demonic
guidance or demonic companions. And at that very moment that the voice (high as a counter-tenor, feminine in
its caress) of Mephistopheles calls him. And the last time
Faust cries out about how he will immerse himself in the
redeeming Work, it is just as he sinks down dead—only
to be reborn (or to have someone be born). He falls and
a young man stands up, sassy as a Blake drawing of glad
youth, and springs away.

With Faust's wave of healing, wave of work, Busoni at
least frees Faust a little from the Christian value system. It
is not the lance that heals Amfortas, no spear, no sword.
Not even the Cup of the Grail—it is the uncontained, un-
containable *water itself*, water in its most active form: the
wave, the overwhelming. It is the pure water itself—water
that the lance can jab and stir but never wound, water
that the cup can try for a time to contain. Water is the
grail beyond the grail. Though letters of grail spell 'a girl,'
and confuse him for most of his life, what he really wants

is beyond any one or any thing he craves. His *désir* on the other side of his *demande*.

Best of all things is water, sings Pindar.

❦

Faust's wager is not with the devil, but with reality itself. His wager is: Let what I have imagined become real. I make reality.

❦

The penis is the only woman a man really has. The foreskin retracting during erection rolls over the glans the way a snug skirt peels off the round hips of a woman. Deep origin of fascination with striptease and unveiling, Salome's dance. Think of Helen veiled in *Doktor Faust*, veiled but *übrigens nackt* [naked, by the way]. The woman who is naked and clothed at once. A woman's body is the real penis, of which the little one-eyed fellow between the legs is just a sad, yearning symbol. When the alchemists (for example Michael Maier in *Atalanta Fugiens*) says "Bring fire to the fire," this is much of what is meant; bring the body to the body.

Dream within dream within desire. More than any music I know (here I think only of the sound of the orchestra and of *her* voice, I forget, if ever I knew, the words in her voice, the words that are just another part of her body's fugue), the sleepwalking monologue of the Duchess of Parma is the sound of someone in love, disastrously, wondrously, in love, drifting by the power of pure desire alone through the sea of what she—she too is an eternal Will! —wants to feel, wants to receive. It is the Duchess, the more or less real-world figure (rather than the fantasized Helena, or the ditzy maiden Gretchen in whom Busoni does not find much to interest him), she, the Duchess, who is the Faust among women, the power and self-delusion of her own "*ewiger Wille*" to feel, love, desire, be possessed.

Balzac says in a notebook somewhere: "Any woman who can no longer be tricked by a love letter is a monster." I think of that as I listen (over memory's ardent but unreliable radio) to the Duchess's long dreamy scena, hearing it already though the actual internet broadcast hasn't yet reached that scene in the opera. The actual is hurrying to keep up with my memory.

The Duchess is Faust's counterpart, the projection of his self-delusion. She is his penis, wandering out of control down a night of desires, encounters, abandonments —however intense the excitement, the penis eventually falls, detumesces. The will sleeps. The penis is the sleep-walker—*La Sonnambula* in yet another opera.

Lacan's sense that the penis only does its work when veiled. It is the veil of the foreskin I want to talk about, no less than the symbolic castration of the penis 'lost into' the woman, the veil of flesh—isn't it Geza Roheim who carries on about the foreskin as the vagina? Woman as veil, Salome dances. For this dance, a man pays with half his kingdom.

In Busoni's manuscript of the text—of course he wrote the libretto himself—(4 Oktober 1917—what else was happening that day? The Battle of Broodseinde, part of that half-year-long massacre called Passchendaele), Busoni writes *ich Faust, ein ewiger Begriff*, then crosses the last word out, writes in *Geist* instead, then crosses that out in turn, writes *Wille*. 'Concept' becomes 'Mind' becomes 'Will.'

Very important this point: the Christian—uncircumcised—Lacan discusses the veiled (preputial) penis. Now link it with and contrast it to the circumcised Freud's insistence on symbolic castration.

Freud seems to locate castration everywhere except in the most obvious wound of circumcision itself. Strange how the early Jewish (but unbelieving) analysts seem to pay little attention to circumcision as an issue. The shyness of Freud? The tacit assimilation? Perhaps Freud's determined resistance to Rank's root doctrine of the birth trauma is fueled not just by Freud's conceptual preference for his 'own' Oedipus complex as explanation, but also by an awareness that *the issue of birth trauma would open the door to a consideration of 'circumcision trauma'*—which immediately introduces (as Freud nowhere seems to allow) a *radical rupture in psychic topography* between male and female, Christian and Jew...naively one wonders how the pain of infant circumcision could possibly fail to constitute trauma—with consequences to follow, if indeed trauma explains anything.

I wish I knew Freud better. What *does* he say about circumcision? I keep thinking he doesn't want to know anything about it, about anything that would so profoundly and incurably separate patients into inalterable categories – isn't a great part of the beauty of the noble construction of his life work exactly his insistence, everywhere implicit, on the unity and integrity of the human psychic organization, same in all people?

ᕱᕀᕟ

Faust, dreaming:
I was always young. It needed no transformation music, pretty as it is, for me to seem so again. My beard and fusty robes sprang away from me the way leaves rush from a lawn, cleaned away by an invisible wind.

"To seem so again." To seem to myself young, and seem so to you. To her.

I was the devil I sold myself to.

ᕱᕀᕟ

And Germany is calling again.

Latin faustus is a contraction of favustus = fortunate, favored, favored by fate.

German *Faust* = fist.

Which do I mean, my force or my fate? Am I agent or am I angel'd?

Spoused fun. Faust pun. He needs a wife I need a wife. What's true for him truer for me. Comparative of bliss.

He goes from woman to woman, not out of licentious-ness but to seek the perfect wife. No matter how many he has. Marriage is no obstacle to married bliss. Find her, whoever she is. Whoever he seems to be.

Gretchen is a nickname for Margaret, Marguérite = *margarita*, 'pearl.' A string of pearls. He finds her, smooth, simple, pale. One after another. The serial infatuation of the empty hand.

Because he is a perfect husband he must marry every-one he meets. Everyone who seems as if she might be the perfect wife.

His desire is the fire in which they're both to be refined. Defined. They are transformed by what he wants. A hoax, like the hoax of poetry.

This is not adultery but its opposite.

This is not infidelity. It is a pilgrimage of faith itself.

Faith is belief in the perfectibility of person, in the per-fectibility of relationship.

Adultery, adultery is settling for imperfection. Settling. It is as when we say of a substance that is not purely itself, it has been adulterated. Something is adulterated when it is not utterly true to itself.

Adulteration destroys the alchemic process. Aborts it. In clear crystal spheres the true essences ripen as colors and hold the colors firm. But in the adulterous alembics the brewed elixir becomes a venom, a sad mistake. He thinks.

And so on Easter morning:

I am a bottle, dark blue glass, barely translucent but translucent.

In me is a message carefully and neatly written, on sturdy paper with decent ink, screwed tight and stuffed into the bottle's neck.

Name, personality, history, so forth—all those are just the cork snugged into the mouth of a little phial.

The red message is intact inside. I am in the sea.

I wait for you, wave. I wait for you, shore.

Certainty was never my business. A puff of smoke, greenish, from my chalice. A few dead leaves, scarlet symmetries. That's sure enough. Enough to go on.

She knew she was in trouble when she felt his eyes all over her body, not just her face. Not just his glances that smooched along her cheeks to linger on her lips. Lips open, moving. To speak. His eyes were on her body. Body: midriff, loins, nape of neck, socket of knee, small of back, hollow of throat, curve of belly, *chute de reins*. She knew she was in trouble when she could feel him reading her skin. Her cautious smile—he had measurements for that. He had a musical notation for her shallow quick breaths.

He stole her feelings. Shanghaied them into his complicated design. There he worked them into the pattern

ROBERT KELLY

→206←

—her feelings, so important to him, as if he had none of his own.

Faust has no feelings. Something to bear in mind.

The autistic will.

His phantom city he built around her. Live in me, he seemed to be saying. But he *had* no in.

A perfectionist has no peace, ever.

He was a pilgrim through a world not yet finished. Never finished. He was to go on. He called that living, sometimes he called that loving.

She was afraid of him, so she took him in her arms. Maybe he would be so close to her that he could not hurt her. Lacking the leverage that distance gives.

She could see him: he studied her the way a blind man faces the rising sun.

She thought: how does what he sees have anything to do with me?

Open me, open me and read! He would say things like that, even the devil could make no sense of such jargon.

The language of enthusiasm is always inexact. If you truly knew the thing you wanted, you would not go on wanting it. Want means a consciousness of deprivation, whereas knowing is consciousness of possession.

Enthusiasm speaks from deprivation, always approximates, blurs, yearns.

The shadow adds dimension to the man. She studies his

shadow in turn, trying to know the thing he makes happen, the thing of which he cannot be fully aware.

No man knows his whole shadow, she said, and he thought her clever for saying so. It made him more determined to possess her. Or not so much possess her, as possess that power which simultaneously summons, appropriates and dismisses all such images into and from the slim chapel in the world, in his mind, that she occupied. Her amber yellow hair.

Faust dreaming:

I am a lover of chastity. I yearn for chastity the way a poor man hungers for money—anxiously, energetically, dreamily, in vain. The metabolic turbulence I bring to my quest for the object of that desire annihilates the very quality I seek.

In the story of Midas his fingers found the same quality in everything, and everything he touched became the same. The same. His so-called gold.

When I touch her, my touch imbues even the freshest virgin skin with my own weary experience, a kind of sour taste that after a moment I recognize as the taste of my own mouth, my sour old kisses, left as defilement on her skin.

I make unclean. Parable of the leper: he goes through the world ringing his bell. In the old dictionary, he is illustrated by a woodcut of a woeful figure tottering along, wearing a huge heart on his shirt. The leper comes along and promises: What I am, I make you too.

Immundus. Unclean. As if: un-world, un-worlded. The world is clean. The only chastity (he is told) is everything that is, left just the way it is. The unclean lover takes his love out of the world. In French *immonde* means sordid, unclean. A world is ordered. A world is what is clean.

❧

Come home with me.

I want to wake and see you beside me on the bed, your head pillowed in the bedding I have left bare for you. I have saved you from the world. I study morning light on your cheek, the stain of shadow along your throat. I hear you breathe. Not meaning to, you have saved me from the world.

There is a strange ancient novel called *The Recognitions.* It begins with a sentence that haunts me all my life: "I, Clement, a native of the City, have been all my life a lover of chastity."

Clement, whom we call of Alexandria, says of himself, I am a native of the city of Rome. I feel utterly known a thousand years before I'm born.

This book translates me. But in vain again. For Clement in the book achieves that which he sought, finds it because he already is it.

Is Socrates wrong, then? Love, far from being penurious and full of hungry wanting, is Love actually all Surfeit and *satis* and serene with its own fulfillments?

He found what he was, and he found it in everyone.

If you must be chaste to find chastity, must I be or become the woman I desire?

Is Faust Marguérite? (No wonder she has little to say for herself. He has all the lines.) Faust looks (and what a sad story this is going to be), he looks for that quality he desires, looks for it in a person who is enough like him to support the inference: 'this person is a lover of chastity,' but also enough like him to warrant a foundational impurity, a looseness, a door somewhere in the back of the house slamming open and shut in the hot prairie wind. Through that portal, unclean lust slouches in and out.

⟨❦⟩

Faust writes on a piece of stiff cardboard: Never doubt your desires or your entitlement to them. Doubt is loud, and others will hear it, and come to doubt you too. Faust looks at what he's written and doubts it too. It seems childish, cynical, adolescent, accidental, merely true.

Faust in his dealings with men and women much prefers civility to truth. Truth changes with situations, while civility is permanent.

Faust in his dealings with angels and demons is much more likely to give and expect truth, imagining (wrongly) that angelic beings perceive situations better than humans, however wise. This is superstition, of course, and will get him into endless trouble.

Angels and devils are in the situation too. Or they are the situation. How can someone in a situation see the whole situation, which itself is part of an endlessly proliferating network of situations. Each situation brackets all the others, and is bracketed in turn.

Faust knows this too, of course, because he's smart. But because he is still a little boy, he believes that telling the truth is the civility we owe to angels. And true enough, it is. It is superstition, however, to expect truth from them in return. Because pure Presence alone is the only civility we can expect from angels, the only gift they have to proffer or withhold.

Faust feels the warm pearls slip through his fingers.

Pearl after pearl. Such a long string of beads. Has he ever counted them? How many pearls is forever? Can he tell the pearls that are his past from the ones that are to come? Pearls of identity.

What if this one warm lustrous pearl in his fingers now, round, sensuous, faintly exciting, between slope of thumb and fingertip, what if this one were the last pearl of all? Would he know he had come to the end of the rosary and started round again? How can he tell? Would it be again if he didn't know it was again?

How warm a pearl is. It never loses a certain animal warmth or spirit. You can tell it was alive once, before it was slain by admiration, desire. By being possessed. It may still be alive. Or capable of summoning (or is it only simulating?) life from the body with which it rests in contact.

Is the warmth coming from the pearl or from the skin? From her or from him? Maybe it is a product of contact itself.

Faust remembers a Russian mystic who taught that the sun gives no light and no heat. Space beyond earth's kindly atmosphere is dark and cold. What we call heat and light are earth's response to the distant diamond icon of the sun. Light and heat are response. They are the friction of earth's love song, earth's welcoming the sun's invisible ardent ray, the spill of glory from the touch of love.

Or maybe earth is just us, ourselves. Maybe heat and light are our answer, billions of humans metabolizing all their lives, marrying the sky.

This heat comes from me, Faust thinks. When he thinks this, all at once it becomes bearable for him to remember that after all is said and done, the pearl borrows its warmth from the skin. As once it borrowed its substance from the tender self-regard of the oyster, the anxiety that spoke and spoke around a core of doubt.

Its luster is its own.

Where does the skin go to get its heat? From the pearl, surely. We feed one another. I am Faust and you are Marguérite, and the other way round.

All the properties of all the pearls are complete in any pearl. A praise of monogamy!

Except for the allness of them. The many. If one were enough, once would be enough. If once were enough, there would only be one sunrise in the world. Then one sundown and no more kisses.

This must be why, on Easter morning, when the bells are danging and the fools of the town, those ordinary people, are putting on their fuzzy pink cloth spring coats and their lime-green sports jackets and their two-tone shoes, Dr. Faust himself is slumped in his armchair, his hands, weary of pearls for a moment, toying with a small blue bottle.

This is the poison.

He doesn't propose to drink it in order to become young again. He is always young again. He can't grow old, he can't grow out of his adolescence, desires, requires, skin and silk and flying through the air, all the Witch Sabbaths that a young man dreams and an old man, he is an old man, can no more stop dreaming than he can stop breathing.

Breathing too is a young man's folly. Hence the bottle. Breath and folly, youth and desire, all can be escaped at once.

But what image will be the last one to form in his mind's eye, clear or murky, looming there as his consciousness, such as it is, dims down for the endless night, dims out, yields, stops. What image last will lurk inside the mind? He remembers asking that question when he was young, eighty years ago he asked it and still he doesn't know.

What is the final image?

And suppose it is her, the last one, the one who still is waiting for his answering letter, the phone call, the promised necklace, the book of Sufi proverbs he borrowed, the weekend in the mountains, all the feints of love? Can he leave her so unsatisfied?

Why should she be more satisfied than I, Faust wants to know. That is crabby and selfish of him, even to think it. He knows that, he unthinks it, the thought turns into Well, at least I can satisfy her, a little, maybe, now if not later, now if not forever.

But he'll have to stay around to do that. He puts down the blue bottle and picks up the green telephone.

☙❧

It is strange, or not so strange that in the West, in love as we are with masks and those who wear them, we have never noticed that all our principal heroes are just different stages, different ages, of the same man.

Don Juan—who has often been the one speaking here—is an immature version of Dr Faust.

And Faust is he now; run out of steam, he can be described as learnèd, *doctus*, doctor. That is, he can be defined by what happened to him, his *hap*. The weary wisdom that accumulated in his heart. It stifled his passion without in the least extinguishing desire.

Don Juan and Faust are respectively the middle-aged and old-aged stages of the young hungry happy hero we call the Grail Knight, *pierce-the-veil*. Parsifal is the larval stage of Faust.

But maybe the man, the hero, does not age at all. His society changes around him. Some crafty angel out of Adorno could tell us, but doesn't it seem that when the chivalric age ends, Parsifal's quest for the Holy Grail makes him a different person, since there is no Christ, no blood, no cup to fill with it, no company of love in the mercantile proto-bourgeois world—Philip II's Spanish Empire, Vermeer's Delft. The Grail Knight must become the Girl Knight and seek out women, who alone remain prized, mysterious, imaginably holy, and who—unlike the Grail—remain multiple, sacred in each instance, each instance compelling to the next, the whole holiness graspable *only when all the instances have been embraced*. Women are many. Manifold as the opportunities for grace in a godly world, manifold as the opportunities for profit in a merchant world.

And then Faust is a very old youth indeed, and the spirit of his quest is alive enough in him to make him uncomfortable with his wise, displeased serenity. Serenity means night music. And he doesn't want to go to bed yet. Not yet.

☙❧

Faust teaches how to relax into ardor. His pupils come up the stairs one by one most days, he embraces them one by one as they come in. Hour after hour, life after life. When they leave they take the wax of his candle, leaving him to keep his flame alive as well as he can. They take the glass of his glasses, the sand of his hourglass, the Christ off his crucifix, the words out of his books, so at midnight he has to pray to an empty wall.

All they leave him is geometry. All they leave him is empty pages and a still keen urge to fill them.

❖215❖

In his discomfort with his stillness, he writes essays on Nomadic Poetics, on the Art of Exiles. He rediscovers in the curlicues of his wet fleshly brain the lost Germanic epic the poet Ovid wrote during his exile among the Goths. He argues that literature reveals its truth best in translation, when it is estranged from what it supposes to be itself and becomes the other, or at least the other's. Undistracted by the sound of its own voice, the smell of its own breath, it is candid in translation.

※

Faust thinking:
I have achieved the transmutation. The work of thirty-seven years has finally, quietly, been completed. The stone. Bred in mind then banished to the world of objects, returns and recognizes itself a subject again. Returns to my body. To be my bones. Every bone renewed. Every integument by which one bone knows another.

Then he takes out a postcard of the Tour Saint-Jacques and turns it over. He writes in Latin on the message half of the card. In translation, he has said: This erection in Paris not far from the Town Hall, the Woman's Cathedral, the River, this upthrust emblem tells much of my story. Stonework, the little lizards who run down from the sun, the girls who make waterspouts of their hands so that the rain says something to the street below. He has room only to sign: *your Faust*. But he does not write anything in the name and address side of the card. He does not know to whom to send it. He turns the card over again and admires, above and on either side of the mysterious tower, the uninflected vivid blue of the sky.

I have achieved the stone. It has come home and claimed me.

I belong to all the things I ever said.

He crosses that out and tries again: I belong to all the things I never made.

Awake now, he gets up with a stiffness in which he imagines he can distinguish the muscular torpor of recent sleep from the clumsy stiffness of old age. He goes across the room, away from the window, and pours himself a glass of liqueur, green pastis, and pours some water onto it, so that the clear emerald green turns yellow and grows turbid. He drinks some of this, and goes back to his chair, balances the glass on the chair arm.

They know my name but they do not call me. I know their names but do not touch them. We are even in our sad desuetude. We are equals.

◦◦◦

Faust puts maps up on his walls—stained, wrinkled, discolored sheets that represent, usually ineptly, the glorious landscapes of the earth that once were women, stayed women long enough for the eye of the artist to observe them, and recognize their lineaments afterwards in the habit of sea and the haberdashery of rock and cloud.

A map on the wall is always a woman in disguise. He writes this and thinks about crossing it out.

Then he fears that doing so will make it all the truer, since the hidden is worth more than the evident, isn't it?

Elle, qui fût la belle heaulmière. The woman who once was beautiful, another man's wife. A woman lost. Or still here, hidden in time. Heart hidden in mocking ribs.

Faust thinks of a woman standing at a window, taking in a view of the city, perhaps giving the city a view of herself. Which comes first, to see or to be seen? How are they different?

Sometimes he sees her as if he were looking up at her from the sidewalk several stories below. Sometimes, though, he is in the room with her, watching from behind, observing what little of the sky and house roofs and steeples is not obscured by the graceful curve of her opaque and curious body.

She stands there against the light. She who used to stand for the light. The only light he needed. Once.

Sometimes he sees her as from a window directly across the street from hers. At those times, their eyes seldom meet. But sometimes they do, and they dare to stare. There, each thinks, that is the one they call the other.

And when they stare, then it is that Faust, not she, is the first who looks away, shy not of the woman (I think) but shy of the sudden suspicion that he is looking into a mirror, and that she is he.

Or that the only woman left to him is the one projected from his eyes.

A woman is a mirror, he writes, and crosses it out.

Maybe she is the only woman he ever knew, even

though he successfully courted one thousand and three of them in Spain. Were they just the several, separate breaths of his sighing, his desiring? Maps, walls, women—all symbols of one another. But of what else?

That too he thinks about crossing out, and does, then realizes—as if a moment too late—that Else is a woman's name too.

He wonders: the poison in the little blue phial, warm from my touch now, a blue pearl, a blue rose of forgetfulness, haven't I drunk it already, many times, haven't I died many times?

And then he forgets. He forgets, just as he has forgotten many times before. Only in forgetting can he go on.

Startles, wakes, starts again. The blue poison is surely my ink. Why didn't I know it long ago? The clear poison took color from the bottle in which it lived so long.

Now he writes the world dead. Word by word.

Death lives in glass.

Faust is almost sleeping now. Blue ink.

I have used this ink to poison the world, infect you. Love letter by love letter, poem by poem, treatise by treatise, I have infected you with my own virus, with me, with me, with the view from my window I made you once, once, think was your own. And in that rapt moment when you knew me as yourself, we lay down together as it always was, became as close to one as two can get

and this love lasted till the light faded from both
    our windows
and all our doors were banging in the wind
and one of us got up to shut them and the other
    was alone
and never came back and still am alone.

Faust is sleeping. The blue bottle rolls out of his fingers
and drops, unbroken, into the skirts of his warm robe that
bunch at the foot of his chair.

Kafka's Brother

‒‒‒‒‒➤‒◉‒◄‒‒‒‒‒

IN THE DREAM I WAS READING a story about a young writing prospect who was writing a story. His story was a simple one, a mystery of the old-fashioned kind, a crime, a detective, a side-kick, some traveling around in an unknown country, a wise old priest, a solution. When he was finished, it was barely long enough, but was long enough, to be a novel, so he set about finding a publisher. But first he showed it to his friend. The friend explained to him all the faults, and suggested ways of correcting them. First of all, the novel, if it was a novel, was badly proportioned—the opening and entrainment of the narrative took too long, the denouement and proffered solution came too soon and were presented too hastily—it felt more like a collapse than a completion. The book had the wrong shape. So it has to be longer. But above all, this novel lacked intellectual and aesthetic significance. "Even in a detective story," he said, "we want more than plot. We want the sense that what we're reading is important. Give us this sense."

So the young writer hearkened to his friend, took back the manuscript and set to work. He darkened his story, deepened the characters, brooded on the landscape, discovered wiser things for the wise old priest to talk about. He found things that actually did seem pretty interesting, about architecture and its effect on churchgoers, about what happens to the soul when people look at trees in autumn, that sort of thing. The young writer was happy, he liked this repacking and embroidering, and soon the novel was twice as long. He showed it to his friend, the friend was satisfied, and said, "This is a really good piece of work you've done."

It wasn't long before a publisher took an interest and gave the young writer a decent contract; soon enough the book was published, the usual trade reviews like *Kirkus* and *Publishers Weekly* were raves, the book found itself in the windows of fashionable bookshops, and had two stacks of itself on a prominent table at every B&N. Sales were impressive, though not remarkable. The young writer walked about in a swoon of delight.

Then the real review came. Big as his ambitions, serious as his novel. Was it in the *New York Review of Books*, or a monthly? In any case, the review savaged the book. It told the writer what perhaps he suspected all along: the plot was compact and intelligible, the characters plausible, the local-color set pieces effective—it was, the reviewer said, a very clever piece of work. It had muscles, good bones, fair reach—but it had no heart. No heart at all. Just clever workshop stuff, a do-it-yourself project with no soul.

So the young writer went home and shot himself. In the head, or the arm, or the belly, but not in the heart. He had learned that he had no heart to aim at. Later that day, an indifferent world received the news of his by now predictable decease.

At this point in the dream, I became aware that the last sentence I had just read was a variation, parody, of the famous last sentence of Thomas Mann's *The Death in Venice*, about the shocked and respectful world receiving the news of Aschenbach's death. I realized that there was more to this sad little story I had been reading in my dream than I thought at first. I began to become aware that the story I was reading actually came from a collection of linked tales, a whole book of them called *Kafka's Brother*. And that the 'friend' spoken of in the story, who gets the boy to spoil his work with false ambitions, is actually the Kafka's brother of the title, the unknown accompanist who guides many generations of young writers unerringly towards illusory public success and profound personal despair.

It is Kafka's brother who whispers big plans, who guides the writer's hands towards plausible solutions and away from the structures of thought and poetry. So it is to escape Kafka's brother that some writers on their deathbeds cry out *Max, burn all my work.*